WHAT BLOGGERS A

RAW HONEY

KNIGHTS OF SILENCE MC – BOOK IV

BY

AMY CECIL

Wow just wow....Amy Cecil has blown me away this time. I went from a quiet unassuming Mom to a MC knights of silence biker bitch in minutes or at least that's how I felt.

- Alison's Blog

Raw Honey is a never boring insight of the Knights of Silence club life. Looking into Honeys life will open your eyes to so many emotions. Beautiful Crazy is the only words to describe this book.

- Leave Me Be I'm Reading

Unrequited love at it's finest! My heart broke for Honey. Amy Cecil has a beautiful writing style that creates beloved characters that pull at the Heart strings.

- This Girls Books

Told in Honey's point of view, we get an alternative look at previous events. She's sassy, she speaks her mind, and she knows what she wants. Cecil has done an amazing job not only in telling Honey's story but in *The Knights of Silence Series*. Very well done!

Amy Cecil has taken Knights of Silence MC to a higher level with Raw Honey and the introduction of the Vitali family. They are about to rock your world. Be prepared to fall in love with Amy Cecil's MC family. I can't wait for more!

I warn you now, Raw Honey will leave you craving for more! *Raw Honey* is solely Honey's point of view. Being able to experience Honey's perspective from the first 3 books and onward really gives the reader an insight as to just about every event that was covered in the books, and it was done beautifully! She toys with your emotions all the while concocting a new relationship you can't help but be compulsively obsessed with!

Another delicious, golden gem by Amy Cecil!! Once this story has been picked up it will be glued to the reader's hand far past the ending. It is a book which will linger, forever loved and begging to be reread always.

RAW HONEY

KNIGHTS OF SILENCE MC

BOOK IV

Badass Bikers, Hot Chicks and Sexy Romances.

KNIGHTS OF SILENCE MC

Suggested reading order:

Ice

Ice on Fire

Celtic Dragon

Forgetting the Enemy

Raw Honey

Loving the Enemy

Sainte

Book cover design and layout by Ellie Bockert Augsburger of Creative Digital Studios. www.CreativeDigitalStudios.com

Cover design features:

- Beautiful and sexy blonde woman with helmet: By Belphnaque / Adobe Stock
- Portrait of strong healthy handsome Athletic Man Fitness Model posing near dark gray wall By halayalex / Adobe Stock

Editing Services provided by Carl Augsburger of Creative Digital Studios. www.CreativeDigitalStudios.com

ISBN- 9781798019160

DEDICATION

*This book is dedicated to my dad. I miss you every day.
You may be gone, but you will never be forgotten.
I love you, Dad.*

AUTHOR'S NOTE

Please be advised that this book contains subjects that may be considered dark and taboo. If you are a reader who is sensitive to certain triggers, then perhaps this may not be the book for you. You've been warned.

CHAPTER 1

Edinboro, PA
Three Years Ago

There was a time, not long ago, when I was not a nice person. I was selfish to the core. I did what I wanted when I wanted and everyone else be damned. But I recently realized that you can only get away with that sort of behavior for so long. Eventually, your past deeds will catch up with you and the old saying rings true. You will reap what you sow.

Six years ago, I left this town and swore I would never come back. I was engaged to be married to my childhood sweetheart and I ditched him at the altar. I could blame it on the drugs...and for the longest time, I did. But looking back, I realize that I was fully aware of my actions and what I had done. All I cared about was my next fix and the night before my wedding, I pawned my engagement ring to get it. Then I left. Then, to make matters worse, a month later I discovered that I was pregnant. I couldn't even take care of myself, let alone a child, so I did the only thing my cowardly ass could do: I had it aborted. It is the number one regret of my life.

I really never thought I would be back. But there is something about a small town, and this small town in particular, that brings me here. I find myself sitting in my car on the side of the road, debating whether I should just plunge in and face my past or turn around and leave.

My name is Amanda Benson, and I am a recovering drug addict.

It took me the longest time to be able to admit that. But now, after many months of rehab, I am proud to say that I am 1095 days clean. That's three fucking years and I am damn proud of my progress.

As I look at my surroundings, I can see the small town of Edinboro before me, just down that hill. To my left is the town cemetery and to my right is the home of the Knights of Silence MC. The property is completely encased in a tall chain link fence and is guarded at the gate. I remember the MC when I was here before, and I wonder if all the members are the same.

When I was here before, I would see the bikers around town and it was apparent that there was a true brotherhood with them. Briggs used to talk about their loyalties to each other and how far they would go to protect their own. *That's where I need to be. Safe and protected behind that fence. But how do I get in without sleeping my way in?*

I'm lost in thought when I hear the low rumble of Harley pipes behind me. Looking in my rearview mirror, I spot *him*. I say that as if I know him, but I don't. I spot a man that even on his motorcycle makes my heart beat loudly in my chest. He parks his bike behind me and cuts off the engine. When he gets off his bike, I can see that he is tall and broad-shouldered, with a thin waistline. He takes off his helmet and his jet-black wavy hair falls loosely around his neck. He begins to walk up to my car—no, actually he saunters toward me—and I roll down my window. Looking in the window, he takes off his sunglasses and my eyes focus on the bluest, most piercing eyes I have ever seen.

"You alright there, darl'n?" he asks.

At first, I am speechless. He's fucking beautiful. He's wearing a black leather cut and his name is clearly patched on the right: Ice.

That must be a nickname. Underneath his name, it reads President. *Holy fuck.*

"Uh sweetheart, you ok?" he asks again.

"Oh yes, I am. Sorry," I reply. "I was just hanging out here thinking."

"Thinking? I can come up with several places to think that are better than this," he says.

And before I know it, I find myself telling him just about everything. I explain to him that I just got back to town and that I left under pretty bad circumstances. I told him that I am terrified to go any further. I have no idea why, but for some reason, I feel that this man will protect me and that all my secrets are safe with him.

"Well, if you haven't figured it out yet, that's my clubhouse over there," he says as he points to it. I nod. "Why don't you come on over and have yourself a drink? Then you can think some more on what you're going to do next."

"Really, just like that?"

"What do you mean?" he asks.

"Well, I thought you had to be a member or the girl of a member to go in there?" I ask.

He laughs. "No, darl'n, we can invite anyone we want."

"Well, I'm not gonna sleep around with your members or you, if that's what you are hoping for."

He laughs even louder. "Sweetheart, I'm only offering you a place to get your thoughts together. But yes, I do have an ulterior motive. I'm hoping to get you off the road. That curve over there is dangerous where you're parked; if a car comes around too fast, they won't have enough time to see you. It could end up real bad for you and I would hate that I didn't do anything to stop it."

Ok, so now I'm totally embarrassed. "Oh, ok ... well, if you don't mind, yes I'd like that," I say.

"Good. Follow me, then." I nod. He puts his sunglasses back on and walks back to his bike. I watch him in the rearview mirror, paying particular attention to his incredibly delicious ass. When he straddles his bike and places his helmet on his head I literally swoon. It's the sexiest thing I have ever seen.

He revs the engine and drives up in front of me. I pull out behind him and follow him to the clubhouse. When he gets to the entrance the men guarding the gate immediately open it. He stops briefly and speaks to one of the guys standing guard and then pulls on through. They subsequently wave me in. I follow Ice and park next to a row of Harley Davidson motorcycles. *Is this a prerequisite? Do they have to ride a Harley to be a member of the club?* I think to myself.

Not sure what to do next, I wait in my car and watch him. He's so fucking sexy. He cuts off the engine and undoes his helmet. Taking it off, he hangs it on the handlebars of his bike. I watch as he dismounts his bike. I love watching him move. Everything is so precise and sexy.

He saunters over to my car and says, "Ready to meet the boys?"

"I guess," I reply. I roll up my window, cut off my engine, and get out of the car.

"Come on, darl'n," he says as he walks toward the door. I quickly follow behind. "We won't bite," he adds and then chuckles.

Holy shit. He's got the sexist laugh I have ever heard. I quickly remind myself, *Get a hold of yourself, Amanda. You are not gonna sleep with him.*

Once we're inside, I'm quite impressed. Well, not with the smell—the whole place smells like stale beer and cigarettes. But the main common area is nice. There is a beautiful oak bar shaped like a "U" with barstools all around it. The room contains three pool tables, video games, and a large flat-screen TV mounted on the wall. In that portion of the great room, there is a myriad of old furniture. Behind the bar is a kitchen, with a large oak table in the center. To the left of the kitchen is a stairway.

There are several members of the club sitting around; some are watching TV and some are at the bar. When we get further inside, Ice walks me over to the bar. One of the men looks up and I immediately know I could like him. He has kind eyes. Ice says,

"This is Hawk. He's our VP and go-to guy. Hawk this is, uh ..." He pauses. "Honey, I'm sorry, I don't know your name."

"It's Amanda," I reply.

"Well, that just won't do. Everyone here has a road name, so what'll we call you?" He thinks for a minute and then says, "I like Honey." He looks at his VP for his thoughts on the matter and Hawk nods. Normally, a name like that would have pissed me off, but coming from him, I like it. No, that's not right. I don't like it—I fucking love it. It's his special name for me.

"Well Honey, it's damn nice to meet ya," Hawk says. I nod and smile. I could really like it here.

"I found Honey on the side of the road just outside the gate. She looked as if she needed a friend." He looks at me and winks. "Darl'n, just make yourself at home. If you need anything, Hawk here is your man."

"Thank you," I reply. Ice starts to walk away and Hawk immediately gets up and follows him. He stops Ice not far from me and they keep looking over to me as they talk. It's obvious that they are talking about me. I am beginning to feel self-conscious and uncomfortable. *I don't belong here. Maybe I should just go.*

Hawk walks back and sits down at the bar. "Take a seat, Honey. Ice tells me that you may be sticking around for a while." He pauses and says, "Can I get you a beer or something?"

I shake my head. "Water would be good, thank you."

Hawk gets up and walks into the kitchen. He comes back shortly with a bottle of water in his hand. "Here ya go."

I take the water from him. "Thank you."

We sit there for several minutes in silence and then Hawk says, "So Honey, what's your story?"

"No story. Just got back into town. That's all."

"So you used to live here?" he asks.

"Yep. Been gone for six years. Just got back today."

"You got family in town?"

"Not anymore. My parents passed away over a year ago. It's just me."

"So if you don't have any family here, why did you come back?"

I can't help but laugh. "I've been asking myself that same question since I got here."

"Sounds to me like you're troubled about something," Hawk states.

I look at him and smile. "Just a lot on my mind."

"Look, Honey, I'm gonna give you some advice. I know, I know, you didn't ask, but here it is. What you choose to do with it is your business." He takes a drink of his beer and continues, "It seems to me that you're not sure if you want to be back or not. I get that. But whatever is holding you back from returning to our wonderful little town of Edinboro isn't worth you putting your life on hold for. Nothing is. Live your life, darling. It's the only life you have."

His words strike a chord with me and I ponder them thoughtfully. He's right. I shouldn't be afraid to face my demons; I should deal with them head-on. But there has always been something that's held me back. But I think that if I hide inside the MC, 'cause hiding is what I do best, it will give me time to face what I need to. *But how do I get myself an in with these guys?* I watch as one of the guys walks behind the bar and gets himself a beer when the idea hits me.

"Hawk, do you all have a bartender?"

"Naw, we just help ourselves."

"A cook?"

"Hell no. Sometimes the old ladies will cook something, but it's a rare occasion. It's a shame, too, because we have an awesome kitchen that is never used."

"Would you like one?"

"One what, darling?"

"A cook?"

"Who? You?"

"Yeah, me," I reply.

"Well hell, I don't know. It's never been something that we've considered, but we're always open to new ideas. Let me run it by Ice and see what he says."

"Really?"

"Yeah, we probably couldn't pay you much, but I bet the guys will tip well. And maybe we could offer you a place to live. We've got a few vacant rooms upstairs."

"Here at the clubhouse?"

"Well, yeah. I know it's not the Ritz, but it's clean and rent free."

"I like free," I reply. Suddenly, I am hopeful. I drove into town dreading it, but now I'm actually looking forward to being back. I can stay hidden away with the MC and I won't have to face my past, for now. It's the coward's way out, but that's exactly what I am.

Hawk gets up from the bar and steps away. I hope that he's going to talk to Ice now.

I sit and watch the other men who are milling about in the common area. I really could call this place home.

After about thirty minutes Hawk comes back. "I talked with Ice. He's open to the idea, but wants to talk to you first. Follow me."

I get up and follow him to a door that is off to the left of the common area. There are two other doors and a staircase. He knocks on the door and opens it without waiting for a response. "Here she is," he says as he gestures for me to walk in.

"Hey, Honey. Have a seat," Ice says. I sit down and he continues, "Hawk here tells me that you are looking for some work."

"Yes, I need a job."

"And you are willing to cook for us poor slobs?" he asks.

"I love to cook, yes."

"Well, this is what I propose. We'll take you on, in sort of a den mother role. You will live here at the clubhouse rent free, but you will not be treated as a sweetbutt. Keep up the bar, cook one meal a day, and ensure the clubhouse is cleaned on a regular basis. I'll pay you $200 a week plus room and board. It's not much, but it's all I can do for now."

I don't hesitate one bit and jump at his offer. "I'll take it." Not having to pay for food or rent would allow me the opportunity to save some money. And being here would keep me away from the shadows of my past. For some reason, this place makes me feel at home. And frankly, having this guy as my boss is a definite plus. "I've got one question, though." I know it's silly, but I just have to ask, "What is a sweetbutt?"

He and Hawk both laugh and Ice replies, "A pass-around. A woman that "services" the guys."

Mortified by his response, but also relieved, I reply, "Oh."

"Well, you did inform me before that you weren't gonna sleep with me, right?" he teases.

"Yes, I did," I reply proudly. *Oh, baby, all you have to do is say the word and I'll be yours,* I think to myself. *But I would never tell him that.*

"Wanna start today?"

"Yes, sir," I reply.

"Hawk, show her the vacant rooms on the other side of the building and let her pick one. Get the boys to help her move her stuff in." He turns to me and says, "I assume you don't have much in your car—unless you have a moving van coming in?"

I laugh and say, "No, just what's in my car. Clothes and shit, you know."

"Gotcha."

Hawk says, "Come on Honey, let's get you situated."

I am so happy I could burst! What started out as a shit day has actually turned around and just may be the best damn day of my life.

CHAPTER 2

I've been with the MC for two weeks now and I love it. Hawk let me pick out a room, which is perfect for me. I even have my own bathroom. I think this place was an old motel that was converted to meet the needs of the MC. All the rooms have their own bath. My room was the biggest vacant one, with a small sitting room that was separate from the bedroom.

The boys in the MC are really nice and are very respectful of me. I understand from Hawk that Ice laid down the law where I was concerned and I'm quickly learning that everyone does what Ice says. I guess that's why he's their president.

I've made friends with a couple of the guys, especially Hawk. He is such a sweet man and not bad to look at either. I mean, he's not Ice, nobody compares to Ice, but he's not bad. He keeps asking me about my past, but I'm just not ready to talk about it with him. Perhaps I should. Perhaps it would make it a lot easier to let things go if I do. Hell, I don't know.

The guys love the meals. At first, only a few guys showed up for dinner and I worried that my value to the club would wane and I would have to leave. But after word spread through the club, just about every member comes in for dinner when they can. It warms my heart to see them eat so heartily and the compliments just make my day. I'm definitely growing on them and absolutely love taking care of them.

Today is my cleaning day, so I have worked my way through the clubhouse cleaning the rooms on my side of the building and the common area. I haven't been in the upstairs portion of the other half of the building, but I guess that will need to be cleaned too. I know that Ice's room is over there and I hope it's ok that I clean it.

I walk up the stairs and get to the top. There's a small hallway with two closed doors. I open the first one. This is definitely Ice's room and surprisingly, it's neat and tidy. I walk over to the other room, expecting to find some type of sitting room, but I see that it's another bedroom. Interesting. This room is spacious like mine, with a queen-size bed on the center wall and a nightstand on each side of the bed. On the opposite wall is a dresser and in the corner is another door, which I assume is a closet, like mine. In the other corner is another door, which opens to a bathroom. It's clear that this room is vacant, which I find somewhat odd. *Perhaps this is set aside for a special guest or something? It's definitely the nicest room in the place.*

In the couple of weeks that I've been here, I haven't seen Ice with a woman and have often wondered why a man like him isn't taken. I make a mental note to ask Hawk about it. I doubt he will tell me anything, so I'm sure I will have to find a way to ask him without it looking like I'm prying. Which is exactly what I'll be doing, but he doesn't need to know that.

I quickly go about my business getting everything on this end of the building cleaned and make my way back downstairs. It's close to dinner time and I have to start getting things ready. Ice gives me a weekly allowance for food so that I can do the grocery shopping on my own and plan out my meals. I really couldn't ask for a better boss or a better situation.

I've just finished getting dinner put together when Hawk comes walking in.

"Whatcha doing, Honey?" All the boys now call me Honey; I love how Ice's nickname for me has stuck. I don't even think that any of them, besides Hawk and Ice, know my real name.

"Just got dinner in the oven. You eating with us tonight?" I ask him.

"Hell yeah. I wouldn't miss one of your meals," he replies and I smile. "Why don't you come and have a drink with me? There's something I want to ask you."

I look around the kitchen and see that everything is ready to go, so I agree. Wiping my hands on my apron, I take it off and lay it on the counter and follow Hawk out to the bar.

He goes behind the bar and gets a bottle of water from the cooler, then pours himself a beer. He doesn't even ask if I want one; he knows that I'd decline.

"So why don't you drink, Honey? Don't like the stuff?"

"No, I like it too much." I contemplate telling him that I am a recovering addict, but then I hesitate. What if he tells Ice and he kicks me out? "I do better with water, trust me," I add. Suddenly, memories of my past begin to clutter my mind.

Three years ago ...

I have not had a fix in two days. "I can't do this!" I scream. Nobody hears me because I am the only person in the room.

I am at the Mountainside Treatment Center in New York City. I finally made the decision three years after I left Edinboro to get myself clean. The abortion put me in a tailspin and over the course of the following years, I kept getting worse. My wakeup call came when I almost died of an overdose and landed myself in the hospital. But it's only been two days...I can't do it.

I quickly remind myself about what brought me here and begin to talk myself down. But these overpowering cravings are fighting to win. I just can't let them. And, if the cravings aren't bad enough, the vomiting, chills, tremors and the never-ending pain in my joints don't make it any easier.

I'm quickly roused from my thoughts when I hear Hawk say, "Still not gonna tell me your story?"

"Nope." I take a drink of my water. "Is that what you wanted to talk to me about?"

"No, actually...well, I was wondering if you'd like to go out on a date with me?"

I look at him curiously. "Why would you ask me that, Hawk? You heard what Ice said, I'm off limits."

"Oh darling, I heard him. You're off limits for a fuck and dump. That's not what I'm asking." He looks away shyly then turns back to me and says, "Look, I think we might have something here and I'm willing to pursue it and see where it goes."

I am completely thrown for a loop. Hawk and I have become friends and I would have to say that he is currently my closest friend, but I've never seen our relationship as anything more than that. I think back over the last couple of weeks and I'm sure that I never gave him any indication that I was interested in more. So why does he think that we have something between us?

"Oh Hawk, I like you. I really do, but I'm not ready to be dating anyone right now. There are things in my past that you don't know..."

"That's because you won't tell me," he quickly interrupts.

"Because I'm not ready to tell anybody, Hawk. It's not you, really, it's me." I cringe inside and think, *Oh God, that sounds so clichéd. But it's the truth. Hopefully, he'll understand and will remain my friend.*

"Ok, I get it. But I'm gonna tell you this: I'm not giving up. There will come a day when you're ready to tell me and when you do, I'll be right here waiting for you."

"Still my friend?" I ask hesitantly.

"Of course. I'm a big enough man that I can get past it when a beautiful woman rejects me. I won't hold it against you."

I give him a hug and say, "You know, you really are one of the good ones."

"Damn straight I am, and it will do you well to always remember that."

"I'm sure you will make sure that I never forget it," I say and he laughs.

The rest of the members start trickling in and I realize I really need to go check on the roast that I put in the oven. I get up and proceed to the kitchen. The roast is progressing nicely, so I return to the common area.

"Hey Honey, when's dinner gonna be ready?" Rebel calls out. "I'm starving."

"Soon, Rebel. Just finishing some things up."

"It smells fucking amazing," he replies.

"Thank you."

We've finished dinner, but Ice never came back to the clubhouse. The boys are in the lounge area watching the football game and I'm at the bar, keeping their beers coming. Hawk sits up at the bar with me; I think he's staying to keep me company.

"You know, you don't have to babysit me," I say. I feel bad because I think that he's here instead of hanging with the guys because of me. "You can go watch the game with the guys."

"I can see the game just fine from here. I normally don't hang with the guys anyway."

"Yeah, I've noticed that." I pause and then casually ask, "So is Ice ok?"

"Of course he is, why do you ask?"

"Well, he never came back after he left this morning and I was worried."

"Oh, no need to worry, he just went home."

"Home? I thought this was his home." I'm completely surprised at this. I never thought he had a home other than this clubhouse.

"It is, most of the time. But he also has a house on Edinboro Lake. His kid sister is in college and when she's home on the weekends, he spends time with her."

"Oh, I didn't realize he had family."

"Just Ari, that's his sister. He's raised her since she was twelve. Tragic story, really. Several years ago on New Year's Eve, his parents went out and were hit by a drunk driver, killing them both. They not only lost their parents, but due to some bad investing by his dad, they lost all their money too. Ice was twenty-four when it all went down."

"Oh, that is tragic."

"Yeah, but once he got hooked up with the MC, things started turning around for him. And the old ladies around here helped him a lot with Ari."

"This really is a family, isn't it?"

"Oh, darl'n, you haven't seen anything yet. But yes, we are definitely one big family." He pauses and then adds, "A lot of the members who have old ladies don't hang around the clubhouse unless we are going on a run or Ice calls church. But about once a month, we do some type of family event where we all hang out, including kids. It's chaos, but so worth it."

"Will I have to cook for this?" I ask, a bit terrified. He's making it sound like I'll have to cook for hundreds of people, and I'm sort of freaking out right now.

"Oh Honey, no. Ice has it catered. It's much easier and everyone gets to just kick back and relax instead of work. You'll see, we've got one coming up next Saturday."

"Well, that's a relief."

"Yeah, it's a lot of fun. And you'll get to meet everyone."

"I'm looking forward to it."

The night continues on without event and by the time I get back to my room, after cleaning all day and cooking, I'm beat. After I take off my makeup and wash my face, I get ready for bed. When I lie down my body goes limp. I think about what Hawk told me about Ice; I can't even begin to imagine how difficult it would have been for him to care for a little sister while working his way up in the club. Hopefully, I will get to meet Ari and we'll be friends.

Hawk mentioned that the guys' old ladies would be at the party next week. I'm glad—I've really enjoyed hanging with the boys, but some female companionship sounds really good.

Eventually, my thoughts begin to wane and I fall fast asleep.

CHAPTER 3

Weeks now have turned into months and I have to say that I don't feel like a visitor anymore. This is my home and these boys are my family. I would do anything for them and oddly enough, I know that they would do anything for me.

I've tried really hard to break down Ice's walls, but I get nothing from him. I've only seen him with a woman once or twice, but never the same woman twice. I never asked Hawk about it before, but today, my curiosity is getting the best of me and I have to know more about him. I've become obsessed with him.

It's late on a Wednesday afternoon and it's just Hawk and me at the clubhouse. Ice and the boys went on a charity run, but Hawk remained here. Last week he sprained his wrist playing basketball out back and won't be able to ride for a while. So it's just the two of us, which means it's the perfect time to probe him for some answers.

"So Hawk, can I ask you something?"

"Yeah babe, what's up?" he says as he takes a swig of his beer.

"I've been here almost six months now and, well, I just find it odd that I never see Ice with a steady girl."

"And you never will," he replies.

"Why? Was he hurt badly at one time?"

"Naw, that's not it. Well, at least I don't think so. He never talks about it much, but I will tell you, he's a fuck-and-dump kinda guy."

"Fuck and dump, huh? You've used that term before."

"Yeah, he's not one to settle down in any type of relationship." He pauses and then says, "Why, you hoping for a piece of him?" I can hear a bit of disdain and jealousy in his voice, so I make a note to answer carefully.

"No. It's just sad, that's all," I reply. *Hopefully, that makes me sound more caring than interested. But shit, who wouldn't be interested? The man is a fucking god! The more time I spend with him, the more I have to fight back the drool that wants to escape my mouth. It's a shame that so much sexiness has to go to waste, because I'll tell you what, I definitely wouldn't kick him out of my bed. But I doubt that I will ever get the opportunity.*

Quickly changing the subject, I say, "So when do the boys get back?"

"Day after tomorrow." Hawk pauses and then adds, "Hey, you know what? There is no reason you should cook for just us two. Let me take you to dinner." Before I can say anything, he raises his hands defensively and says, "Just as friends. I just wanna give you a night off."

"Sure, that sounds nice. Thank you."

Dinner with Hawk was very nice; he was a perfect gentleman, ensuring that our "date" was simply platonic. He tried again to get me to open up about my past, but I'm still not ready. But even though I'm not ready to talk about it, I can deal with it better these days—I have even ventured into town more, not worrying about who I might run into. I guess that's always been my biggest fear—running into Jack, the man whose engagement ring I pawned and ditched at the altar. I've hurt many people, but Jack is the one I hurt most. I'm just not ready to face him yet. But I know there will come a day when I won't have a choice.

Several nights later, after everyone returned from the charity run, Ice is working late in his office. All the boys have either left or gone to their rooms, leaving the clubhouse quiet and dark except for the subtle glow from Ice's door. After I clean the bar, I go to his office to see if he needs anything before I turn in myself.

I knock and he answers, "Come in." As I walk through the door, he says, "Hey, Honey."

"Hey, I was gonna turn in for the night. Is there anything you need before I do?" I ask.

"What time is it?" he asks in surprise.

I look down at my watch and say, "2:30."

"Holy shit. I didn't realize it was so late."

"You've been working in here all night."

"Yeah, I know, just trying to figure out some shit." He pauses and says, "You know what, I'm done for the night. Can I buy you a drink?"

"Uh, Ice, we have a fully stocked bar."

He laughs. "I know. I was making a joke."

"Oh. Sorry," I reply, feeling really stupid.

"It's all good. Come on, have a drink with me."

"Ok."

He gets up from his desk and walks over to the door and I follow. He sits at the bar and I go behind it. "What'll you have?" I ask.

"Makers, straight up, love." I pour his drink, grab a bottle of water, and walk around the bar to sit with him.

"So Honey, you've been with us what, six months now?"

"Yeah, close to that."

"Do ya like it here?" he asks.

"I do, Ice, I really do. All the men have been really nice to me. I've met some of the old ladies too and I like them. It feels like home."

"Good, I'm glad. I know the boys really enjoy having you around." He smiles that brilliant smile of his. "None of them have tried anything, have they?"

"Oh no, they have been perfect gentlemen," I reply.

"That's good. If anything changes, you be sure to tell me."

I nod. "I sure will."

"So what are you hiding from?"

Why is everyone so concerned with my past? Every time they bring this shit up, it makes me remember things that I have long since chosen to forget. But like clockwork, my mind begins to remember, again.

At first, during my experimental days, it was the euphoric high and the surge of energy that I would get from the coke that made me want it. Then it got to the point that I not only wanted it, I needed it. And now, after four days in rehab, I still need it...and I can't get it. I'm not strong enough to make it through this. I can't do it. I should have died when I overdosed. I don't deserve to live.

"Uh, Honey?" I'm suddenly taken out of my daze and I look at Ice, who is looking at me like I've grown a pair of horns.

"What?"

"What are you hiding from?" he asks.

"What makes you think I'm hiding?" I reply defensively.

"Oh Honey, you can't fool me. You spend every minute of your time inside this clubhouse, except when you go grocery shopping. And when you do, it's always late in the evening. You're avoiding something or someone."

"I am."

"Talk to me."

I realize that I can't hide anything from him and I shouldn't. This man gave me exactly what I needed when I got to town and I owe him the decency of being honest with him. I take a breath and say, "Well, I'm a recovering addict. Before I left town, I was engaged to be married. The night before my wedding I pawned my engagement ring for a fix and left him high and dry. I have not spoken to him since and really don't want to right now."

"Does he still live here?" he asks, never mentioning anything about the revelation that I am a recovering addict.

"Yes, he does. Actually, you know him."

"I do?" he says, surprised.

"Yeah, it's Jack Briggs."

"Get out!" He takes a drink and looks at me. "Really?"

"Yeah. That's why, for the couple of times that he's been here, I retreat to my room. I'm not ready to face him yet. It's bad enough that I left, but then I had his unborn child aborted. It was an awful time in my life." *Don't go there, Amanda. Do not let those memories surface,* I quickly remind myself. I can't break down in front of Ice.

"Fuck, Honey, that sucks. I'm really sorry, hun." He nudges my shoulder and says, "You'll be able to face him when the time is right."

God, I love this man. I say, "I know." We're both silent for several minutes and then I say, "You didn't mention anything about the addiction thing, or the abortion."

"No, I didn't."

"So it doesn't bother you?"

"Look, Honey, everyone has a past. We've all done things that we're not proud of. But I can see that you are truly trying to change your life around and I admire that. You're on the right course and I would never hold your past against you."

"You really are something."

"What do you mean by that?" he asks.

"It's just that I have never met anyone like you. You're a big, strong biker dude, president of this MC. You're demanding and hard...but at the same time, you're one of the most understanding and kind guys I have ever met. You're one in a million, Ice. Don't ever forget that."

"Oh, baby, if you only knew. But thank you."

"So how long have you been president?" I ask. I've wondered about this for a while now, but it never seemed to be the right time to ask.

"I was voted in as president about three months before you came."

"That's it? I thought you'd been president for a lot longer."

"Oh really?"

"Yeah. So what happened to the guy who was president before you?"

"He was killed by a rival MC."

"Oh no! Which one?"

"The only one that gave us problems, the Satans. But I quickly took care of that."

"What'd you do?"

"Let's just say that they crawled back into their hole after I was done with them. Hopefully never to be heard from again."

"Oh."

Ice drinks the last of his bourbon and then looks at his watch. "Well darl'n, I think I'm gonna call it a night. Thanks for keeping me company."

"Anytime, Ice," I reply.

He gets up from the barstool and turns to me. He leans down and kisses me on the cheek and says, "You know, Honey, you'll always have a home here."

It's a good thing I'm still sitting because I can feel my legs go weak. *Fuck, it was just a kiss on the cheek.* A little breathless, I reply, "Thanks, Ice, I appreciate that."

As he turns and walks away, everything inside me is screaming to follow him and offer myself to him. Lord knows I want to, but I know that would ruin everything. I take a few minutes to get my wits back and then get up, turn out the lights, and head to my room.

More memories of my past begin to consume my mind.

I'm still at the rehab center and I'm now fifteen days clean. I made it through most of the detox and now I am just dealing with the everyday urge to use again. I am told that they won't release me until I am clean for two months. God, that seems like such a long time. But they say that first they heal the mind, then the body. I never knew the drugs took such a toll on my physical well-being. My body needs hydration, so they make me drink ungodly amounts of water every day. They are constantly checking my meals, ensuring that I am eating nutritionally balanced food. And they allow me to sleep as much as I want, which is the best part of all this. I'm so fucking tired every day.

CHAPTER 4

"Happy Gotcha Day, Honey!" Rebel exclaims as he comes down the stairs and enters the common room.

"Gotcha Day?" I ask.

"Yeah, it's two years today that we gotcha."

"Oh my God, Rebel, really? You couldn't come up with anything better than that?"

"Hey, I worked hard on that. And at least I remembered."

"Well, there is that." I sigh. "Wow, two years." It's hard to believe; I really can't imagine my life without my boys. "I'm surprised that you even remember that."

"Well, it's easy for me. I came to the club just a few months before you, so your gotcha day and my gotcha day are close."

"Oh, I didn't realize that."

"Yeah, I was sent here from Ireland by my parents. My uncle was the former MC president."

"The one that was killed by the Satans?"

"Yeah."

"Oh, I'm sorry."

"It was hard to swallow finding that out when I first got here, but I helped Ice avenge his death and somehow it seemed to make it a lot better."

"What did you guys do?"

"Now Honey, you've been with the club long enough to know we don't divulge club business to our women."

"Yeah, I know," I say, disgusted. I never asked Ice about what he did and I was really hoping that Rebel was gonna tell me. *Damn, these boys are tight-lipped.*

"Well, I gotta run. Have a good day, Honey."

"Yeah, you too, Rebel." He grabs his keys and gets up from the barstool and heads for the door.

The club is having a big family gathering tonight and I'm so looking forward to it. Hawk was right, they are a lot of fun and I really enjoy spending time with the ladies.

The party has been going on now for about four hours. The kids have all been sent home with babysitters and everyone is kicking back, drinking, and having a good time. I swear I am the only one not drinking tonight. But that's ok. I'm still enjoying myself.

Now don't get me wrong, I still find it hard to be around all the booze and there are times when it really annoys me as to how much they drink. I guess annoy is a harsh word, as I realize that I am more jealous of their ease with their alcohol consumption. For me, the temptation is always there and I struggle with it every day. But I knew that would be part of my recovery and I know that each instance that I don't drink only makes me stronger.

A few of the members have left, but most of them are still here. We're all hanging out in the back of the clubhouse, near a huge fire pit with a raging fire. Some of us are sitting around the fire, others are milling around talking. Ice and Hawk are off to the side, deep in conversation. They keep looking over to me and it makes me curious. I walk over to them and say, "Hey guys, can I freshen those drinks for you?"

"No thanks, Honey, I'm good. Besides, you aren't supposed to be working during these parties," Ice says.

"I know, but you know how I am. I can't help it." They laugh. *What is so funny?* I wonder. They both seem off to me, which makes me even more curious than I was before.

To my surprise, Hawk walks away abruptly. *What's his problem?*

"Was it something I said?" I ask Ice.

"No, Honey, more like something I said, I think. But he won't admit it."

"What's that?"

"Awww no, nothing to worry your pretty little head about."

I'm frustrated because I have a feeling that this has something to do with me, but I have no idea what it could be about. I decide to go talk to Hawk. When I catch up to him, I say to his back, "Hey Hawk."

He stops and turns back toward me. "Hey." His tone is short, which worries me. I feel like I must have done something, but I don't understand his anger.

"Got a minute?"

"Yeah. What's up?" He sounds reluctant, but I'm not going to let him off the hook. I'm gonna get to the bottom of this.

"I want to know why you are so upset."

"It's nothing, darling."

"Don't tell me that. I can tell by your tone and the fact that you walked away back there that something is upsetting you."

"You know what, Honey? I am upset. But I am not going to tell you why."

"But ..."

"No, stop. I'm not gonna tell you why because you should already know. But it's too late anyhow. Ice is my prez, my brother, and my best friend. I will not go against him." He rakes his fingers through his hair. "You don't know a lot about me, darling, but I'll tell you this: I've walked a thousand miles to get here and I don't make any excuses for myself. I left my family when I was still young and never went back for reasons that I won't go into. I made a family of a different kind here, just like you. I have seen all kinds of things, including death. I know I can't stop the train wreck that is about to happen, and frankly, I'm not even gonna try."

"What are you talking about?"

"You'll see," he says and turns and walks away.

I want to run after him, but I have learned not to press and so I keep my mouth shut. I turn to walk back toward Ice. "How'd that go?" he asks.

I shake my head and say, "Hell if I know."

I turn to leave and Ice calls back to me, "Why don't you stay and keep me company? We can people-watch."

I turn back to face him, "People-watch?"

"Yeah, I do it all the time. It's fun."

"Well, I've noticed that you spend a lot of time always off to the side, on your own. You really don't like to mingle, do you?"

"Nope, I'm not a mingling kinda guy."

"I see that."

We spend the next couple of hours hanging out together, people watching. And Ice is right—it's fun. We spend most of the time laughing and when the last of the members leave, it's just Ice and I. We're now sitting by the fire, and the embers are beginning to fade. It's really late. The conversation lulls and it's starting to get chilly. I get up from the chair and say, "Well, I think I'll turn in."

As I start to walk away, he grabs my hand and says, "Stay with me." My heart jumps to attention. *Is he asking what I think he's asking?*

I stop walking and turn back to look at him curiously. He's still holding my hand. "Ice?"

"Stay with me," he repeats.

I still have no words. I think, *Just say what you want!*

He must have heard my silent plea, because the next words out of his mouth send tingles all down my body. Ice says, "Look darl'n, I know I said you would stay hands-off, but fuck, I want you." He gets up from his chair and moves in close. "Your fucking perfume has been driving me insane all night." He leans in and kisses me on the neck, then moves his lips so that they linger right behind my ear. His breath is gliding across my skin, causing goosebumps all the way down to my toes.

Everything in me just wants to melt in his arms, but my self-respect is at stake. Although it pains me to say what needs to be said, I do it anyway: "I'm not a fuck-and-dump kind of girl, Ice."

He backs away and looks at me curiously. "Fuck-and-dump?"

"Yeah. Hawk told me that you don't do relationships and that you are a fuck-and-dump guy."

He laughs. "Fair enough. You're right, I don't do relationships. I've spent the majority of my adult life waiting and I'm not so sure I want to wait anymore."

"What are you waiting for?" I ask.

"Nothing you need to know about."

"I don't know, Ice. Part of me wants to, but the other part of me is afraid."

"Afraid that tonight will be it?" he asks and I nod. He rakes his hand through his hair and says, "Look, I won't make you promises that I can't keep. But I will promise you this—tonight won't be a fuck-and-dump night."

Like a love-sick fool, I agree. *What have I just agreed to? A world of heartache!* my subconscious quickly reminds me. Ice turns to leave, taking my hand and leading me back into the clubhouse. I follow him up the back staircases and directly to his room. *Holy fuck, this is really gonna happen!*

Once we're inside his room, he closes the door behind him and walks over to me. I'm wearing a short jean skirt and a low cut V-neck t-shirt and flip-flops. "Take off your shoes," he says. I slip out of them and he wraps one arm around my waist, pulling me close. He begins backing me directly toward the wall. Once I have nowhere else to go, his hands slip beneath my skirt and he cups my ass. He moans and says, "You're wearing a thong. I fucking love thongs."

I have no time to think or answer, as the only thing that is on my mind is how his hands burn on my ass. He pulls me against him. Dipping his head against the top of my shirt, his lips brush against the swell of my breasts. I sigh breathlessly as pleasure rockets through my body.

He pushes himself up against me and I can feel his erection pushing at my core. He lifts my arms above my head and holds them up briefly while he stares down at me. "You are a beautiful woman, Honey," he says, then adds, "You look ..." He hesitates while he still continues to lock his gaze with mine. "You look sexy as hell like that," he finally says. He then trails his hands down the sides of my body as he moves in to kiss me. My arms instinctively wrap around his neck as I pull him closer. My insides are all fluttery and I feel as if I am freefalling. His hands roam all over my body. He hungrily caresses and digs at my skin. I'm panting when he pulls away from our kiss. He reaches again under my skirt and yanks my panties off, ripping them to shreds.

He moves his hand between my legs and rubs his finger directly against my opening. I moan breathlessly. "I can't decide whether to bend you over and fuck you or suck on this," he says as he slides his finger inside.

"Oh God, Ice, I can't take anymore," I cry out. He swiftly lifts me up as if I weigh nothing and carries me over to the bed, setting me on the edge. Before I can utter another word, he kneels before me. *Holy fuck. Ice, the President of the Knights of Silence MC, is kneeling before me.* The power that it affords me is exhilarating. Hiking up my skirt and moving my legs to drape over his shoulders, he leans in and begins to lick my pussy. He starts slow, teasing me, but then picks up the pace. His tongue is relentless against my clit and I can't help but cry out his name as pleasure shoots through my body. My orgasm comes quickly and he moans, not stopping until I do. It's too much. It's delicious, and I want more.

He crawls up on the bed and kisses me. I can taste myself on him and it's so fucking sexy. I reach down and grasp the button on his jeans, pulling and tugging to free him. Getting the button undone, I then reach for the zipper and tug it down quickly. All the while, his lips never leave mine.

"Wait," he says. He gets up from the bed and removes his jeans. He then opens the drawer to his nightstand and pulls out a condom and sheaths himself.

Oh fuck, I didn't think of that. Thank God he did. He then leans down and pulls my skirt off. He crawls back up on the bed and I have to touch him. I reach down and begin to caress his balls. He moans in pleasure. I grab onto his dick and guide him to me. I have to feel him inside me and I can't wait any longer.

I arch my back to meet him as he pushes inside me. He's fucking huge and his dick stretches my walls, but it feels so fucking good. I'm so wet, but I need to adjust to his girth. "Your pussy feels so good, love," he says. If I wasn't all flesh and bones, I would melt right here and now. He begins moving inside me, burying himself deep.

"Oh, God," I cry. "Harder! Please!" I beg.

He obeys, pounding relentlessly into me. I'm being fucked like I have never been fucked before, and I know that no other man will ever compare to this. I scream as pleasure fills my body. I cum hard and fast, but Ice doesn't stop. He hisses as he continues to pump inside of me until he finds his own release. "Aww fuck, Honey!" he says as he falls on top of me.

Aww, fuck is right. That has got to be the best sex I've ever had. He gets up from the bed and walks into the bathroom, I assume to remove the condom and clean himself up. A few minutes later he comes back with a washcloth and to my surprise, he begins to clean me as well. *Yep, I'm in love and my heart is going to break. I'm fucking doomed.*

When he's done, he goes back into the bathroom and closes the door. He says nothing and suddenly I feel like I don't belong here. His lack of words at this point when I need affirmation the most leaves me feeling that I have just been used. It was the one thing I was warned about and I wanted to avoid. Holding back tears, I quickly get up from the bed and get dressed. Just as I'm about to leave, the bathroom door opens.

"Where are you going?" he asks.

"Back to my room," I reply.

"Ok," he says.

I know I made the right call. As soon as the door closes behind me, the tears begin to fall. *Thank God everyone else is in bed. It's bad enough I have to do the walk of shame, but it would be even worse if it was in front of the entire MC.*

As I walk through the dark common area of the clubhouse, making my way to the other side of the building and my room, I hear a low voice say, "I told you so." I turn back and see Hawk sitting at the bar in the dark with only the glow of his cigarette for light. I didn't know he smoked, I've never seen him smoke until now. There is a glass of what I assume is bourbon sitting in front of him. He's right, he warned me...and I'm too embarrassed to offer a response. I now know what he meant by train wreck. I nod and turn back toward the stairs and go to my room.

CHAPTER 5

What I totally expected to be a fuck and dump with Ice actually turned out better than I thought. We've been fuck buddies for a while now. He said that he's grown tired of the sweetbutts and wanted someone more consistent. He's told me several times that this is not a relationship, but he calls me his "goto girl." I know it sounds slutty, but I'm hopeful. The sex is amazing and I keep praying that he will see that I'm the girl for him. I've been with the club for three years now. It becomes more and more a home for me every day. Well, until today.

Earlier, a woman in hysterics appeared at the gate, saying that she needed to see Caden. I have no idea who Caden is, but obviously Ice knows, because she's in his office right now crying. *I bet this Caden guy is one of the members and got this girl knocked up, so now she's coming to Ice for help. But why would he help her? Does he know her? Maybe she's a cousin or some other relative.*

Just then Rebel comes out into the common area and says, "Tiny and Honey, Ice wants to see you."

We walk into his office and I see the girl in question sitting in one of the chairs across from his desk. Her eyes are all puffy, but underneath her tears, she's absolutely stunning. I'm instantly jealous and I want to know who the fuck this woman is and how she knows Ice.

Ice says, "Emma, this is Tiny and Honey. Tiny will go back to your place with you to get your things. Just the necessities, please; we don't have room for your whole fucking bathroom." He pauses and adds, "Once you get back, Honey will get you set up in one of the rooms upstairs." He then looks at me and says, "The room next to mine will do."

I nod as my heart slowly begins to break. In the three years that I have been with the MC, nobody has ever used the room next to his. Why now?

As if my heart wasn't already breaking, Ice adds, "Boys, spread the word: Emma is off-limits!" I stand there, unable to move. I don't understand what's happening. Ice bellows, "Tiny, get moving." I jump and quickly scurry from the room.

A few minutes later, I see her and Tiny leave Ice's office and subsequently the clubhouse. Hawk walks up to the bar. "What's going on?" I ask.

"Haven't gotten all the details yet, but it looks like this Emma chick is gonna be a guest here for a while."

"Yeah, it does."

"What's the matter, Honey girl? Jealous?" he asks sarcastically.

The tone in his voice makes me feel uneasy and defensive. I say, "No, of course not. Just curious." I pause and then add, "By the way, who's Caden?"

He busts out laughing and suddenly I'm embarrassed because I feel like I should know. "It's Ice. His name is Caden Jackson."

"Oh. I didn't know." My heart sinks even further. I really don't know how much more of this I can take. Before I say anything else, I decide that I need to talk to Ice.

I wait a few minutes and then proceed to his office. His door is open so I just walk in and stand there waiting for him. His brow is furrowed and he looks agitated. I'm worried about him. After a few seconds, he looks up and sees me standing there. He looks annoyed.

"Ice, are you ok?" I ask timidly. *I want to know who this Emma girl is. I want to know what her being here means for me.*

He always said that I could always call this place home, but now I'm not so sure. I feel threatened and I don't like it. All of these questions fill my head, but I'm too afraid to ask any of them.

He smiles and says, "Yeah, I'm ok. This business with Emma just has me on edge, that's all." I want more, I need to know more, but he's not volunteering anything. Then he says, "When Emma gets back, I'm counting on you to make her feel welcome. She isn't familiar with our lifestyle and has many misconceptions about us. You need to help her understand. Are we clear?"

"Yes, Ice, I understand," I reply and inside the knife that stabbed me when she got here has now turned inside my chest, its ragged edges shredding what's left of my heart. *Ask him!* my subconscious screams.

But I can't. Instead, I ask, "Just so I am clear, you want me to set Emma up in the room next to yours?"

He looks annoyed again and I'm afraid that I have just overstepped my boundaries. "Yes, you are correct." And then he basically dismisses me, saying, "If you would go now and get things ready, I would appreciate it."

I leave his office as he asked and it takes everything in me to keep a brave face on. The tears want to fall, but I will not let them. They can wait until I am alone, in my room. The rest of the members start coming into the clubhouse and head straight for the chapel. Ice must have called a meeting.

When Emma and Tiny arrive back at the clubhouse, Tiny takes her on a tour while I watch her. Who is she to Ice? I can't believe how jealous I am right now and I don't even know her. I have no idea what she means to him, but it must be something special, because he's turning this fucking club upside-down for her.

When Tiny takes her up the back steps, I can't take anymore. I run from the common area and go straight to my room. The tears start busting through just as I get to my door. I throw myself on the bed and begin to cry uncontrollably.

After several hours go by, I decide that I need to pull myself together and go back downstairs. I need to get dinner ready. I make my way down and when I get to the bar I see Rebel and Tiny sitting at the bar. I go behind the bar and ask, "Refill?"

Rebel slides his glass forward and says, "Sure thing, Honey. Thanks." Just then Ice comes walking in. I didn't even know he'd left. He comes up to the bar and asks Tiny, "Emma all settled in?"

"Yes sir," he replies. "I even carried her bag in for her, so I assume she is upstairs unpacking her things."

"Good, thanks. There are a few bags in the Jeep, please bring them in and put them in my room." He then turns to me and says, "Pour one for me? I sure could use one."

Tiny gets up and heads out to get the bags that Ice mentioned while I pour Ice his drink. He looks over at Rebel with his shot in hand and says, "Drink is the feast of reason and the flow of the soul." He downs the shot while Rebel looks at him curiously.

"What?" Rebel asks. "Where do you come up with that shit? Drink being a feast and flowing into the soul ... what the fuck does that mean?"

"Hey, don't knock Alexander Pope!"

"Who the fuck is Alexander Pope?" Rebel asks, laughing at him.

Ice shakes his head and says, "Never mind. I don't have the time or the patience to explain it to you. I'm going to check on Emma." Rebel continues to laugh as Ice leaves.

"What's for dinner, Honey?" Rebel asks me.

"I have no idea," I reply, "But I'm sure I'll come up with something. Which reminds me, I need to get to it." I leave the bar and head for the kitchen.

I look at the clock, which reads 1:30. *Good. That's plenty of time to get a roast in the oven.* Some of the old ladies are coming tonight, so I want to make something a little more special than normal. I get it prepared and in fifteen minutes, it's in the oven. I whip up some mashed potatoes, some broccoli, and a salad.

When dinner is ready, all the boys and the old ladies come in and sit at the big table. I absolutely love these family dinners. We're all seated, getting our food when in walks miss prissy pants wearing a tight pair of skinny jeans and black halter top. And the freaking bitch has heels on. *What the hell? She looks amazing.*

I watch her as she stands in the doorway as if she's waiting for a formal invite. It's so obvious that she doesn't fit in with us. We're what-you-see-is-what-you-get kind of people; we're all down to earth and we definitely do not put on airs. She is the exact opposite. She will never fit in. I think about making a good show by inviting her in, but Ice beats me to it.

"Emma, come have some dinner," he says as he gestures at the empty seat next to him. She walks in and hesitates. He shakes his head and says, "Darl'n', it's ok, please sit. If you wait any longer there won't be any food left." She sits down and I almost choke on my food when I notice the way we are seated. Ice is in the middle and the two women that love him are seated on each side. It's a fucking triangle. I happen to glance at Hawk and he smirks. He sees it, and I'm sure everyone else at the table does too. Ice fills up her plate with more food than she can possibly eat and then says, "Eat up. The roast is really good."

I watch her curiously as she takes her first bit. She smiles and then says, "This meal is amazing!"

Before anyone can say anything, I make it quite clear who made the meal by responding to her statement, "Thank you."

Ice looks over to me and I realize that it is the first time that he has really acknowledged me since Emma came here. Every other time, he was telling me to do something or brushing me off. He gives me that sexy smile and says, "You've outdone yourself tonight."

I can feel the blush rise in my cheeks and can't help but smile back. In that one look, he just briefly banished all my insecurities. I nudge his shoulder teasingly and say, "Thanks, Ice. I aim to please;

you know that." I look up at Emma and see that she actually looks ill. *Oh yeah, she's definitely in love with him.* She begins to pick at her food and suddenly I feel very triumphant.

After dinner, some of the guys remain seated around the table talking, while others disperse to the common area. Emma gets up and proceeds to excuse herself. I was fully expecting Ice to remain with the guys like he always does, but I'm shocked when he too gets up and says, "I think I'll join you." She smiles at him and I want to reach across the table and scratch her eyes out. She then looks directly at me as if to say, "checkmate." *Fucking bitch!*

I watch as they walk out of the kitchen. When Ice tenderly places his hand at the small of her back, my heart drops. In that instant, I know I've lost him.

Emma finally went to bed. Ice, Hawk, and Rebel are meeting in Ice's office. I want to see if they need anything, but I know the rules: stay out of club business unless you're asked to be involved. Several hours go by and finally, Rebel and Hawk leave Ice's office. I really want to talk to him, so now that he's in there alone, I make my way to the door. I'm about five feet from the door when it opens and he comes out. He spots me and says awkwardly, "Goodnight, Honey." As he turns to go up the stairs, he adds, "Wonderful dinner tonight."

"Thanks, Ice," I say proudly feeling much more secure in our relationship. "Goodnight," I add, but he's already at the top of the stairs and I know he didn't even hear me. As I turn to head to my room, I hear a scream. Quickly turning back toward the staircase, I begin to rush up. Halfway up the stairs, I hear laughing. I stop and wait to see if I can hear anything. After a few seconds, I hear laughter coming from both of them. *I really have lost him, if I ever had him at all.* I turn and proceed back down the stairs and make my way to the other side of the building and my room.

CHAPTER 6

After a sleepless night, I find myself downstairs early. I'm not an early person and thoroughly enjoy my sleep, but I have so much fucking shit on my mind right now, I wonder if I will ever sleep again. The bar needs a good cleaning, so that is where I find myself this morning. It's better if I keep myself busy; somehow it doesn't hurt so badly. Aw, fuck, who am I trying to kid, it hurts like hell. Sometimes, I wish it had just been a fuck and dump with Ice. It would have been so much easier in the long run.

Just as I'm wiping down the bar counter and trying not to show all the fucked up emotions I am feeling, Emma comes down the back stairs. *Fuck! Just my luck. The last thing I want to deal with this morning is her, especially alone.*

"Good morning, Honey," she says shyly as she approaches the bar.

Do I intimidate her? I wonder. I reply shortly, "Morning." I then continue to go about my work. If I show her any type of kindness right now, I won't be able to control the tears. And the last thing I want to do is be a crying mess in front of her. She will never see my hurt.

"Do you know where I could get a cup of coffee?"

"Coffee is in the kitchen. If you want cream or sugar you will have to find it; me and the boys drink our coffee black and strong." I know I'm being rude, but I want my message to be crystal clear:

You are not welcome here. She nods and heads into the kitchen and I breathe a sigh of relief.

A few minutes later she comes back into the common area with her coffee in hand. Apparently the princess is not quite as helpless as she appears. She sits at the bar. *Oh fuck. Please don't talk to me*, I plead to myself. *I can't carry on a conversation with her. I won't.* Luckily, she drinks her coffee quietly and doesn't try to engage me in any conversation.

As if they could hear my plea, Tiny, Doc and Dbag come down. As soon as Tiny sees Emma, his eyes light up. *Fucking traitor! I think I need to have a talk with our sweet, boy-next-door prospect. Surely he knows not to mess with Ice's girl.* As soon as I think that, the realization hits home—"Ice's girl" doesn't refer to me anymore.

"Good morning, Miss Emma," Tiny says, then continues, "Have you met Dbag and Doc?"

"No, I haven't," she replies. She looks at the other two men and says, "Nice to meet you, I'm Emma."

So fucking polite. They both eye her up and down and smile. They don't say anything to her, just smile and walk away. After they step away I go back to cleaning up the bar.

Emma asks Tiny, "I was wondering—if you are not too busy, would you be able to take me to my apartment? I forgot to pick up my laptop and would really like to get it."

He nervously replies, "I'm not sure that's a good idea. Ice told us you were not to leave for any reason."

We all know that, Ice made it perfectly clear that she was not to leave. Even I heard him say that.

"Oh, Tiny, it's ok. I told Ice last night that I needed my laptop and he said fine. He knows that I was going to ask you to take me back to my apartment."

Tiny shrugs and says, "Well, if Ice okayed it, just let me take care of a couple of things and then we can go."

She gets up and I'm pleasantly surprised when she picks her cup up and takes it into the kitchen instead of leaving it for me to clean up. When I walk in behind her, I see her washing it. When she's done she turns, smiles at me, and leaves. Fifteen minutes later, she and Tiny leave the clubhouse.

Ice and some of the boys had an early meeting this morning, but now they have come back. They're all hanging at the bar, and of course, I am getting them their drinks. Just as I turn to give Ice his bourbon, he asks, "Have you seen Emma this morning?"

As much as I love him, I'm still pissed at him for doing this to me. It's obvious that he has cast me aside, but he hasn't even got the balls to tell me. Then he's all sickie sweet to me and it makes me want to punch him. Knowing that that's not an option, I reply with very little emotion, "She came down earlier and got some coffee. Then I saw her leave with Tiny."

Just as I expected, he looks pissed off at that news. The question is, however, is he pissed at me or at someone else? Well, fuck him if it's me. I may have to swallow my pride and accept this fucked up situation, but I sure as hell am not gonna walk around here all bright-eyed and bushy-tailed.

"Where the fuck did they go?" he yells.

Ok, so he's not pissed at me. Wishful thinking, I guess. He is fucking clueless about anything that I am feeling.

I shrug. Fuck him. He's the president of this club, let him figure out where they went. I'm not his information person. I know I could easily tell him where they went, but he is making my life a living hell right now and watching him suffer a bit actually makes me feel a little bit better.

"Ryder, get Tiny on the phone and find out where in the hell he took her and tell him to get her back here ASAP. And so help me, tell him if anything happens to her on his watch, I'll have his head, not to mention his patch."

"You got it, Ice," Ryder says and he picks up his phone to make the call. He steps away from the bar while he talks and then a few minutes later he comes back and says, "Well boss, it seems that Emma wanted her laptop. Tiny took her back to her apartment and said he was bringing her right back."

Ice turns to Spike and says, "Back them up. I have a bad feeling about this." Spike nods and immediately gets up and leaves.

Ice is acting as if Emma is in serious danger. Could that be why he is being so cautious with her? I don't know the whole story as to why she is here, but if her life is in danger, then this is where she needs to be. Maybe I was too quick to judge her. Still, that doesn't explain the sexual tension between them. We've all felt it.

After Spike leaves, Ice is on edge. He keeps staring at the door as if he is willing them to return. He paces for a while, then sits back down and has another drink. He's drinking more than normal and I begin to worry. Finally, his phone rings and from the conversation, I'm sure it's Tiny.

"You sure as hell fucked up! What part of 'she never leaves this clubhouse' did you not understand?!" Ice yells into the phone. He pauses and then yells again, "Tiny, if you don't fucking get her home ASAP I swear to God you'll have a lot more things to worry about than a tail." He pauses and then says, "You better believe it won't happen again. Get the fuck home as soon as you can!" He disconnects the line and begins to pace again. I don't think I have ever seen him this like this. He's always calm and collected; he never loses his shit. But if he has to wait much longer for them to get here, he definitely will.

Ice keeps staring at the door when finally, Spike comes strutting through the door, cool as ever. It's obvious that he's pretty fucking proud of himself, knowing that he probably saved Tiny and Emma from the tail that Ice mentioned earlier. He's followed by Tiny, who can't even look Ice in the eyes. I'm sure Ice will deal with him later, but right now, his eyes are focused on the door as Emma walks in. She looks like she has been through hell, and for a brief moment, I feel for her. I can't imagine the feeling of being followed by someone that I feared, which I'm pretty sure is what's going on.

Emma rushes toward Ice as he gets up from the barstool and moves toward her. He pulls her into a loving hug, and every bit of empathy I felt for her drains from my mind. I hate her.

"Caden," she squeals, "you are shmooshing me!" He laughs heartily, but I'm just confused. I didn't find her words funny and I can't understand why they are laughing. It must be an inside joke or something that I am not privy to.

"I can't breathe!" Emma exclaims and then I can see what's about to happen. The thing that I had hoped I'd never have to witness. The thing that I have been dreading since Emma came here. The mood in the room suddenly changes as the sexual tension between Ice and Emma burns through. The heat in their eyes as they stare at one another is all-consuming, and every one of us in the clubhouse has stopped and is now watching them. He pulls her close against his body and kisses her. It's not a brotherly or friendly kiss. No. This is an all-consuming, passionate kiss. As I watch the man I love kiss another woman, I realize that he's never kissed me like that. He's never expressed that much passion with me. I can't take any more of this and I run from the room, straight into the kitchen.

I don't care if they see.

I can't hide my feelings any longer.

Oh God, I need a drink! Everything in me fights the urge to march back over to the bar and pour myself a shot. I make myself take another step toward my room and with every step thereafter the urge diminishes.

When I get halfway up the stairs, the last thing I hear is Ice say, "We will discuss today's ordeal later. Church in an hour. Round everyone up." He pauses and then adds, "I'm not finished with you. Stay put." That must have been directed toward Tiny.

As if my heart hasn't broken enough, I hear him climbing the back stairs and I'm sure that he is going after Emma.

CHAPTER 7

About an hour later I'm back at the bar when Ice comes back downstairs. All the boys are in the chapel waiting for him. When he gets to the bottom of the steps he doesn't say a word, he just goes straight into the chapel and closes the door.

I decide that I am speaking with him tonight. I know I have lost, I knew it the minute she arrived, but I need to hear it from him. I will make him face this one way or another. I busy myself getting their shot glasses ready. It's a common practice when they finish with their meetings for each member to come out and have a shot. I never understood that. Those meetings must be pretty stressful.

About forty-five minutes after the meeting started, Emma comes back downstairs. *Why can't she just stay in her room so I don't have to look at her?* I look at her and see that she has been crying, and I immediately want to help. But then I remember who she is and how she has turned my life upside down in just twenty-four hours, and I decide that she can fend for herself.

When she gets up to the bar, she says, "Excuse me?"

I ignore her. I can't even look at her, I'm just not ready. I know that when I do, I will see Ice's lips fused with hers and I will lose my shit.

"Honey, may I please have a shot of whiskey?"

Whiskey? Now that fucking gets my attention. Without looking at her, I reply, "Coming right up." I place her drink on the bar as the boys adjourn from their meeting and head straight for the bar. The last one out of the room is Ice. He pauses at the door and scans the room. I know he's looking for Emma. When he sees her, he makes a beeline directly for her.

"What are you drinking?" he asks her with a mischievous smile on his face. He seems amused that she isn't drinking her usual foofoo drink.

She ignores him and picks up her glass and downs her shot. Slamming it down on the bar, she turns toward Ice and says, "Whiskey." Then she looks over at me and slides her shot glass toward me. She says, "I'll have another one."

I just nod. I am surprised by her boldness. She is pushing his buttons now; she is clearly stating that she is not going to take his shit.

Ice bellows, "No! She will not have another one, Honey."

I immediately stop pouring her drink. She looks at him in disgust. *Oh fuck, this is gonna be good.*

"Cade, I want another drink!" she demands. Just like that, Ice backs down and nods to me. I finishing pouring her drink and bring it to her. She picks up her second shot and downs it, again slamming the glass down on the bar.

"Holy shit, Emma. I never knew you drank the hard stuff." Apparently he's no longer mad; he's acting as if he is proud of her drinking like this. Then he asks, "Why are you drinking?"

The defiance in her response makes me take a step back. "I can drink if I want to. I'm a grown woman, Cade. I'm not a child anymore."

"Calm down there, sweetheart, I was just asking. It's not like you to be drinking hard liquor in the middle of the afternoon."

"How would you know what I'm like? You haven't seen or spoken to me in eleven years. I've changed, Cade. There are a lot of things I do now that I didn't do before. Get used to it."

Are they fighting, or is this foreplay? I really can't tell.

"Emma! Stop! Now!" he says angrily. It's obvious that he's pissed off by her defiance and the fact that she is calling him out in front of the club. Even I know that's a big no-no. "If you don't stop now, I'm gonna take you over my knee." Finally, she stops baiting him and shuts up.

It's lucky for her that she got the hint when she did and shut up. She asks me for another shot, downs it, and then leaves the bar, heading straight for her room. I know she is not a regular drinker, so three shots of bourbon are going to make her feel pretty good in about fifteen minutes.

Right after Emma left, Dbag comes out of the back room and approaches Ice. He says, "I got an ID on that black SUV."

"Whatcha got?"

"SUV is registered to a Mark Grayson. He's a big-time attorney, works in Erie. Lives here in Edinboro."

"You got anything else?"

"Well, I think I might have found something, but I don't know. I searched both the DMV databases and the crime databases. An incident report showed up about the chick's disappearance. Emma's friend."

He looks at him in surprise. "What?"

What the fuck is going on? Some of the pieces are starting to fall into place, but I'm still so confused.

"Well, apparently, the same black SUV was noted on the report. There weren't any details as to how or why it was there. It was just arbitrarily listed on the report as a vehicle involved, but with no evidence tying the SUV to her disappearance. I'm not sure, boss, I've never seen a police report like this one before."

So that's what is going on with Emma. It seems that she's got a friend that is in trouble. And who is this Grayson guy? Boyfriend or fiancé maybe? If she has one of those, that could be good news for me.

"Dbag, I want you to find out everything you can on Mark Grayson. And when I say everything, I mean everything! I want to know how many times he pisses in a day! You got me?" Ice says.

"Yes, sir!" He quickly heads to the back office. A few minutes later, Ice leaves and heads for the back stairs.

He's only been gone for a few minutes before he comes back looking a bit disappointed. He comes up to the bar and takes a seat. I ask, "What'll you have, Ice?"

"The usual, please." I grab his bottle of Maker's and pour him a drink. He finishes it and asks for another.

When I bring it over, I say, "You look troubled. Is there anything I can do for you?"

"Naw, sweetheart, I'm good. Just got a lot on my mind."

After a few minutes go by, the other brothers that had been lingering around the bar disperse, leaving me alone with Ice. *I guess now is as good as time as any. I don't know if I will ever get a chance like this again.* "Ice, can we talk?" I ask. He looks at me, pleading with his eyes to not push this conversation, but I can't let it go. I need to know once and for all. I need the truth.

Looking defeated, he shrugs and says, "Why don't you take a break? We can talk in my office." I smile, finish putting some of the bottles away, and then follow him to his office.

I walk in and close the door behind me. As soon as we're completely alone, I run into his arms. "Ice, I've missed you so much." It's my last attempt to salvage anything between us. I can feel him attempting to push me away, but I just grab on to him tighter. I'm afraid to let go. I'm afraid that this is all we have left. I know he is strong enough to remove me and I appreciate the fact that at least he's allowing me this. After several seconds in his arms, I ease up on my grip and he gradually steps away.

Suddenly, I feel more lost and alone than I did before. But instead of saying the words I know he will say, I hang on and ask, "What's wrong?"

"Honey, I'm sorry, but I can't. We had fun, but it's over," he says.

Tears well up in my eyes. I was expecting this, but that doesn't make hearing it any easier. "But why?" I ask. *He better fucking tell me the truth. Yeah, sure, I don't want to hear it...but if he gives me some bullshit story instead of what is plain and clear, I swear I will never forgive him.*

"Honey, I'm sure you knew this was coming," he states matter-of-factly.

"But, Ice, I thought ..." I don't finish. The hope is gone and there is no point in trying to salvage something that isn't there. He's right—we had fun. But he has no idea how much I love him. He has no idea that I would do anything for him and his club. He doesn't understand that he's my savior and that my loyalty to him runs very deep.

"Honey, Emma and I have a history. I need to see where this—whatever this is between us—is gonna go. I'm sorry if I hurt you. It was never my intent. But you knew from the beginning I was not in the market for an old lady."

I nod sullenly. "I know, I was just hoping ... well, that maybe ... oh, never mind." I turn toward the door, and then look back at him and say, "We had fun though, didn't we?"

He smiles and says, "We sure did." As I open the door, he calls out after me, "Honey, you know you always have a home here. You take care of my boys and me like nobody else. If that's what you want, that will never change."

"Thanks, Ice. That means a lot to me." I turn again to leave and then add quietly, "I hope things work out for you and Emma. You deserve to be happy." Oddly enough, I believe I mean it. He was right, he would have never been able to give me what I wanted from him. Not in the long term. Especially if he's got this history with Emma; that would have always stood between us.

"Thanks, Honey. I hope you find some happiness too."

I leave Ice's office, wiping the tears from my face. Although I have been dumped, I feel that a load has been lifted from my shoulders. I no longer have to worry about trying to please him, or being afraid that he will leave me. I no longer need to worry about where I stand with him. I had never realized how heavily that constant worry weighed on me. But the weight is gone. I walk out to the bar area and see Hawk sitting there alone. He knows where

I've just come from, and by the look on his face, he knows the outcome. He warned me about this a long time ago and I refused to listen.

I walk up to the bar and sit down next to him. Leaning my head on his shoulder, I say, "Wanna drink?"

He looks down and smiles at me. "You were busy, darling, so I helped myself." He smiles at me and his understanding of my predicament is written all over his face. "You look like you have been through the wringer. Wanna talk about it?"

I smile sadly. "No, I don't. But I'd love the company."

"You got it, love. You know that." He puts his arm around me and pulls me close. "For what it's worth, I'm still waiting." I put my arms around him and squeeze.

"Thank you, Hawk. You've always been rock solid for me." I pause and say, "I still need some time, but I promise, I won't forget."

We sit like this in an awkward yet surprisingly comfortable silence. No more words need to be spoken between us. I have no idea what is going on in Hawk's mind, but my mind is closing a Chapter and considering a new one. I will not shed any more tears for Ice or for what might have been.

After Hawk leaves to take care of some club business, I decide to go into the kitchen and just chill to get my thoughts together. After sitting there for roughly an hour, in walks Emma. *You can do this,* I tell myself. After my conversation with Ice, I know that I have to be nice to her. If I start to cause problems, there is a good chance that Ice will make me leave. I have nowhere else to go and I can't jeopardize that.

"Hey," I say as she walks in. She just groans. I think the effects of her drinking are taking their toll on her. I get up and get her a cup of coffee; she's gonna need it. I set it down on the table and she smiles kindly and says, "Thank you, Honey."

We sit there in silence for several minutes before Ice comes bursting in. The look on his face is ashen. I am sure seeing us together has got him worried, especially after the talk we had earlier.

"Emma, I need to talk to you," he says.

"Cade, can it wait, please? I've got a splitting headache and would love to finish my coffee."

"Nope, can't wait. Bring your coffee. My office, now!"

He's being very stern with her and it almost pisses me off. *Can't he see that she is hungover and just needs a minute? Holy fuck, am I actually sticking up for her? Absolutely not. I don't sway that easy. But I will give her some advice.* "Emma, you better go. Ice isn't used to waiting for anyone." She nods and gets up from the chair, taking her coffee with her as she leaves.

CHAPTER 8

The first couple of days after Emma arrived were the worst days of my life, but now I'm just living through a series of bad days because of Emma. Each day, the hurt gets a little easier and each day I try to be a little nicer to Emma. And she has been coming around too. She always offers to help me—at first I didn't want her help, but now it's not so bad. She really is a nice girl, and it's not like she came back to destroy my life. She needed Ice, just like I needed him. Who could blame her?

This morning I woke unusually early after a solid sleep. It's really the first good night's sleep I've had since hurricane Emma arrived. I get myself dressed and go down to the common area. I'm sure I can occupy myself with something useful instead of lying here thinking. Nothing good ever comes of that; it's better to keep myself busy.

I walk into the kitchen and I am surprised to see Ice brewing coffee. "Ice, you're up early."

"Yeah, got shit to do today. Coffee's still hot. I'll be in my office if anyone is looking for me."

He leaves the kitchen and me in his wake.

And that is how things are between us. I guess it's a good thing. He's keeping his distance for me and I know that. But sometimes it makes things so hard. We used to be able to talk, but now I'm just one of the guys. I used to be special.

I get the feeling that the club has got something planned where Emma is concerned. Obviously, I'm not privy to what it is, but I pray that nobody gets hurt. However, I can't shake the feeling that my prayers will be unanswered.

I'm still working in the kitchen when I hear Ice talking rather loudly in the common area. Walking out, I hear him say, "Hey boys ... well, it is official. I've finally found a woman who will put up with me and all of you sorry losers." He gestures toward Emma and continues, "My beautiful, sexy, and smart Emma. She has always had my heart and my protection. Now she has my patch."

I knew this was coming. I expected it. But why does it still hurt so much? I really don't want to hear anymore, so I quietly go back into the kitchen.

Several minutes later, Ice calls for a celebratory drink and of course, I come back out. It's 10:30 in the morning, but they all have their drink. When the drink is over, I start cleaning up their drink glasses. Ice walks over and I say, "Want me to take care of getting her vest and patch?"

"You'd do that?" he asks, surprised.

"Of course I will."

"You're a true champ, Honey. You really are," he says and then walks away.

Over the next week, Emma and I spend a lot of time together. I hate to admit it, but we are actually becoming friends. I like her. She's not a princess. She's got tenacity and spunk, and I love the fact that she doesn't take any of Ice's bullshit.

Ice and the boys have been busy, and now I know why. Emma told me everything about her friend Brianne and her ex-fiancé Mark. It's some pretty fucked up shit and I definitely would not want to be in her situation. But if anyone can get it all fixed for her, it would be Ice and the club.

Emma and I are talking over coffee in the kitchen when we hear a lot of commotion in the common area of the clubhouse: doors banging and lots of yelling. When we step into the doorway from the kitchen, we see that Ice, Rebel, and Ryder have returned, and not one of them is looking very happy. They walk in and head straight for Ice's office. He's barking orders as he comes through, and the last thing we hear is, "Church! Now!" Emma looks over at me. She can see the worry on my face; we both know that something bad has happened.

"What do you think is going on?" she asks.

I shake my head and say, "My guess is that their meeting with Skeeter didn't go very well. Ice does not hide his emotions very well when he is pissed off."

"What do you think happened?"

She's worried. Hell, we both are. Without answering her, I turn to go back to the kitchen and Emma follows. I stop by the sink and turn to face her, saying, "Hell if I know, Emma. These boys try to do good, but they always seem to get themselves caught up in some shit. It could be anything."

"Maybe we should go find out," Emma says.

"No!" I yell. "Women aren't allowed. We do not participate in their meetings and we definitely are not privy to what they do, even old ladies. The quicker you learn and accept that, the easier things will be for you."

Emma and I finish up in the kitchen and head out into the common area. I begin to work around the bar, getting it ready for tonight. Emma offers to help and I agree. She is really growing on me. Just as we finish, the guys emerge from their meeting and head directly to the bar. When I see them coming, I proceed to get their shot glasses out and start pouring beers. When they get to the bar, the first thing they do is down their drinks.

Ice leans over the bar, kisses Emma's cheek, and says in her ear loud enough for me to hear, "We need to talk."

"Ok," she replies sheepishly. She gives me a wary look and then follows Ice to his office.

Later that night, Emma clues me in to everything that has been going on. Apparently, her life is in danger and Ice is sending her away. It's probably the best thing for her. I know she's scared, but Ice is right. The further away from here she is, the less he has to worry about her. He won't be able to function like he's needed to if he is constantly worrying about her safety.

The next morning, Emma and Ice come downstairs and Ice is carrying her bag. She must be leaving today. I wonder, *Is he going with her?* But when I see Ice talking to Rebel, I realize that he is not. Rebel is taking her. She doesn't look happy, which I completely understand.

After Rebel and Emma leave, Ice goes into his office and stays in there for several hours. I almost go check on him several times, but each time, I think better of it. I know if he needs something he'd ask. I just feel so helpless; I wish that there were something I could do to help him.

I should have remembered the old saying "Be careful what you wish for." Three days later, Hawk tells me that Ice wants to see me in his office. I've kept to myself, and I've even been nice to Emma, so I know for a fact that I haven't done anything wrong. But still, I'm curious. It's very rare that he asks to see me in this capacity.

I walk over to his office and step in the doorway. Lightly knocking on the open door, I say, "Hawk said you needed to see me, Ice?"

"Yeah, why don't you have a seat?" he replies. I sit down and look up at him, concerned. He says, "Honey, you've been a part of this club now for many years. You've been loyal to the club and that has not gone unnoticed. You are an asset to this club and every brother loves you. You have cleaned up our bloody messes, our drunken brawls, and have made sure we have decent meals to eat."

Ice looks frustrated, which makes me start to question my conclusion that I have not done anything wrong. I ask, "Ice, have I done something wrong?"

"Honey, no, it's nothing like that." He pauses and then adds, "What I am getting at is that we have never involved you in club business. We never wanted to. Not because we didn't trust you, but because we didn't want you to get hurt. But unfortunately, the time has come that the club needs you."

I sigh with relief and say, "You know I would do anything for the club. I came to you beaten and broken, and you and the club took me in. You gave me a roof over my head, a home, and more importantly, a family. You just name it, I'll do it."

"You might not feel that way when you hear what we need."

"Ice, just tell me. Quit beating around the bush and just spill it." I hate when he tries to sugarcoat things. He's got to know that I'm in for the long haul and that I would do anything for him.

"If you haven't noticed, you resemble Emma."

Well fuck, of course, I've noticed that. Why do you think this whole situation has been so hard to swallow? I know that I was a substitute for her.

He continues, "Emma is in danger. That's why I sent her away. But we need the Satans to think that she is still here. We need them to stop looking for her. Basically, we need a decoy. That's where you come in." I take a deep breath, waiting for the rest. "The boys and I think that from a distance, dressed in the right clothes—and if you straighten your hair a bit—you could be a dead ringer for Emma."

"Where will I be the decoy? Will I be in danger?" I ask.

"You'll be right here at the clubhouse. We're having a party Saturday night. We are tipping off the Satans that Emma will be here, and you just need to stand in. I cannot imagine that the Satans would make a hit on the clubhouse, especially since all the old ladies and children will be here. So, I believe you will be safe. But as both you and I know, there are no guarantees."

"Will you be with me?" I ask.

"Yes, I will."

"Why do I feel that there is more?" I can tell he is avoiding telling me something and it's pissing me off.

"You are a smart woman, Honey. Yes, there is more." He takes a deep breath, and continues, "We need to be convincing. Do you know what I mean by that?"

"I think I do. But maybe you should spell it out for me. You know, so I don't make any false assumptions."

"We will need to be on display during this party. Lots of public displays of affection: kissing, perhaps even running off together leaving the assumption out there that we want to be alone. Can you do that?"

"Do I have time to think about it?" I ask.

"Unfortunately, not a lot. I can give you a couple of minutes now if that will help. I'm sorry for putting you on the spot like this, but we need to act on this quickly." He pauses and then adds, "I know we have some history, and I am guessing that this could be difficult for you; I don't want you hurt."

You already have. I sit there and think about what he's asking. He's never asked me to do anything that involved club business. And I know he's desperate to keep Emma safe and it looks like I can help. Before I change my mind, I blurt out, "I'll do it."

His blue eyes sparkle as he smiles at me, and I melt. *Why does he still get to me that way?* He gets up from his desk and walks around and kisses me on the cheek. *Oh God, I miss him.*

"You are an amazing woman, Honey. One day, one of these boys is gonna be very lucky making you their old lady."

I want it to be you! my heart cries silently, but I know that will never be. He truly loves Emma and the sooner I accept that wholeheartedly, the better off I will be. Maybe he is right, maybe there is someone out there for me—and then I remember Hawk's words: "I'll be waiting."

I can't fight back the tears any longer and my eyes begin to well up. I say, "You think so, Ice? You really think there is someone out there for me?"

He pulls me into his arms and hugs me. "I sure as hell do. Someone better than me."

Before I know it, Saturday is here. The party is tonight. To say that I'm nervous is an understatement. I have questioned myself for doing this many times, but each time I remember that it's for the club. It's for Ice and Emma, and even though my jealousy wants to rear its ugly head, I fight it. I'm better than that and this is my chance to prove it to the club, but more importantly, to myself.

Ice and I went searching in Emma's room to see if she left anything behind. We found a pair of skinny jeans and a simple black shirt and black boots and it all fit perfectly. It's definitely not my style, but I guess that's where Emma and I differ. I've just applied the finishing touches to my face, and as Ice instructed, my hair is straight. I run a brush through it and I'm ready to go. *Perfect. I really do look like her.*

It's after 8 pm and the party has already started. I make my way downstairs and I notice that Ice keeps staring at the steps. As soon as he spots me, he smiles. I can see the relief on his face. When I get to the bottom, I walk directly to him and he says, "Ready to get this party started?"

I smile and say, "Let's do it." We make our way outside so that we can be seen, since most of the attendees are already outside. I guess he's assuming that the Satans are out there somewhere watching the compound.

As we walk, he leans over and whispers, "You look great!"

I beam. I'm glad that he thinks this is gonna work. Me? I'm not so sure. I reply, "Thanks!"

As the evening progresses, we continue to talk and mingle with the guests. Around 10:45, Ice's phone beeps. He looks down and then leans in and says, "Showtime. You ready for this?" I nod and he immediately pulls me close. He begins to nuzzle my neck and kisses me right behind my ear. I can't help but giggle. *God, I love it when he does that.*

We walk over to some other brothers and their old ladies hanging around the portable bar that was placed outside. We talk with them for a while and then I turn toward Ice and slide my arms up against his torso and latch them together behind his neck. He hesitates briefly, but my look quickly reminds him why we are doing this. Ice is not a cheater, so I am sure he is dealing with some pretty harsh demons right now. Then, the look on his face changes and I can see that he has overcome his issues. He leans in and kisses me. The kiss is nice, but it doesn't have the passion that we once shared. It's in this moment that I realize that it would have never worked between us. Suddenly, the dread I had been feeling up to this point is gone and the whole charade gets easier.

We continue to carry on like a couple who are very much in love. As time passes, I can see that Ice is getting antsy. Finally around 11:45, we decide to make our departure and head for the bedroom as planned. About 15 minutes after we leave the party, Ice's phone beeps. Looking at his phone, he says, "Honey, we're good. The Satans left. You can head back to your room now."

I admit that I am disappointed. I was actually having a lot of fun. "Ok, if you don't need anything else."

I walk to the door and just before I turn the knob to leave, he calls after me, "Hey." I turn back to look at him. "You did great tonight. I know this wasn't easy for you. Thanks!"

I smirk and say, "Actually, Ice, it was a lot easier than I thought." I step through the door and then add, "But it's over now. Goodnight, Ice. Sleep well."

I know he thinks I'm hurting and doesn't understand. But that's ok. I'm better now and life is going to be better as well.

CHAPTER 9

The next morning Ice left for the safe house. Some of the boys helped me clean up after the party and now we are just sitting around watching TV.

It's a lazy day and we all just lie around doing nothing as the morning turns into the afternoon—until Ice comes back. Taking us all by surprise, he storms into the clubhouse barking orders. He's frantic and pissed, and I have no idea what's happened. The boys jump and start doing his bidding. He's ranting and yelling and pacing and...fuck. Just fuck. What the hell has happened?

When Spike comes out of Ice's office, I can't keep my mouth shut. I ask, "What happened?"

"They took Emma," he says sadly.

"Oh no!" I exclaim. "But how? I thought she was tucked away and the party last night...I mean, I thought it was all good?"

"Apparently not. I don't know anything else, but it's bad, Honey. Real bad."

An hour or so goes by and everything happens so fast. Ice comes running out of his office yelling, "Get everyone out! Now! It's a bomb!" He begins checking all the rooms and calls over to me, "Anyone upstairs?"

"No," I yell back. "Ice, everyone is out. Let's go!"

He follows me out the door and within seconds of us reaching the parking lot, the building blows. Ice grabs me and holds me down while debris from the clubhouse drop around us. When everything goes quiet, he gets up, brushes the debris off himself, and pulls out his phone. He stops for a minute, looks around at what used to be our clubhouse, and then dials. I have no idea who he is calling or what is happening. I hear him say, "Message received. You got me."

He disconnects the line and turns to me. "Call Hawk. Tell him what has happened here and that I've found Emma. He'll know what to do." I'm so confused by everything that just happened and I want him to tell me what's going on. But he doesn't. He just says, "I have to go," and then turns to leave.

Oh no, totally unacceptable. He can't just leave me hanging here. Not after all this. I call after him, "Ice, wait!" The tears begin to well in my eyes because I have this sinking feeling that this is gonna be the last time I see him. I hesitantly ask, "Where are you going?"

He walks over to me and kisses me on the forehead. "Now don't you go worrying your pretty little head, darl'n. I'll be back."

I stand there amidst all the rubble and for the first time since I found the MC, I have no idea what to do. I feel lost and alone and can't move. My heart is shattered into a thousand pieces and I am worried about Ice. *Where is he going? Is he putting himself in danger to rescue her?* Any other time I would be cheering him on to make the rescue, but if it means losing him in the mix, I'd rather keep him. He can leave Emma with that psycho asshole. We can't lose him.

I suddenly realize that Ice is counting on me. I pull out my phone from my pocket and dial Hawk. He answers on the first ring. I say, "Hey, big shit just went down. Nobody's hurt. The clubhouse, however, didn't survive the bomb."

"Bomb?! What the fuck, Honey!" he yells. "Are you sure you're alright?" he asks.

"Yes, we are fine."

"What the hell happened?"

"I don't know. One minute we were all in the clubhouse hanging out, and the next minute Ice came running out of his office telling us to get out and that there was a bomb."

"How bad is the clubhouse?" he asks.

I look around. "It's bad, Hawk. Real bad. Part of the building is still standing, but the other half of the building is completely demolished. There is nothing but stone, broken-up wood, and glass shards everywhere."

"Fuck. Where's Ice?"

"He left."

"He left? Why the fuck did he leave?"

"I don't know, but he asked me to give you a message."

"Ok, what's the message?"

"He said that he found Emma and he's going to get her. He said that you would know what to do," I tell him.

"Aww, fuck!" he says into the phone. "You stay put. I'll be right there," he adds and then disconnects the line.

It's two days later and we're still going through the rubble grabbing anything that we can salvage. There hasn't been any word from Ice. I've asked Hawk if he's heard from him several times and he just sadly shakes his head. We have no idea at this point if he is dead or alive. *Please let him be alive. It's bad enough seeing him with another woman—who, I might add, is the cause of all this mess—but if he's dead I know for a fact that I will not survive it.*

Briggs came by and filed a report about the explosion. I conveniently make myself scarce when he's around. He is the last person I want to see. I'm still a coward. One of these days, I will face him and do what needs to be done. I will tell him everything and apologize. But right now, I just can't. I'm not ready to face all that now. I just can't.

As we're digging through all the shit, I hear a car pull up. I look to see who it is and when she gets out of the car I am totally shocked and surprised to see that it's Emma. *She's alive. She's fucking alive! Does this mean that Ice is alive?* She stops and talks to Rebel and then after a few minutes, Hawk starts to walk toward her. Maybe she has the answers that we all have been waiting for. I want to go and see what she has to say, but I hold back. I know Hawk will tell me if there is something that I need to know.

I continue to look for anything that we can salvage. But every chance I get, I look over at Hawk, Rebel, and Emma to see if I can gauge what is being said. Then I see Emma faint and fall into Hawk's arms. I rush over as he lifts her and carries her to the club van. Rebel opens the back and he gently lays her down inside.

"What happened?" I ask as I get to the van.

"She fainted," Rebel replies.

"I see that, but why?"

"I told her that Ice was dead," Hawk replies.

"Oh fuck!" *That means Emma has no idea where he is or if he is alive. Damn her. He can't be dead. He just can't.*

Hawk tries to revive her and when she finally comes to, she looks lost and bewildered. She asks, "What happened?" as she starts to sit up. Just then Rebel's phone rings and he steps away and answers it.

"Emma, I don't know much more than you do." Hawk looks over at me. "Honey saw him last, and most of the information I've gotten has been from her."

She turns to me. "Where is he? What happened?"

Reluctantly, I reply, "I don't know. He was frantic trying to find you. He was on the phone in the clubhouse when he realized there was a bomb that had been planted and he yelled for everyone to get out. When he was sure that everyone was out of the building, he and I were the last two out and then the building blew. We all just stood in disbelief for what seemed like an eternity. After he was sure everyone was whole, he made a call. I don't know who he called. After he finished the call he walked over to me and told me to tell Hawk what had happened, that he'd found you, and that he had to go."

"Did he say anything else?" she asks with a note of irritation in her voice. I look at Hawk to make sure that I can tell her more. He nods.

"He said that he would be back."

"Then you all are wrong!" Emma exclaims. "You all think you know Caden, but you don't. None of you know him like I do. If Caden Jackson says he will be back, then you can be damn sure he will!"

"Emma, you are not seeing the big picture here. I think I know him pretty well. The man I know would have taken care of his business and then returned to his club where he was needed most. He wouldn't have left us to pick up the pieces without him." Hawk rakes his hand through his hair and says, "Emma, I know what you're feeling, sweetheart. I want him here too; he was my best friend. But I think you're grasping at straws, trying to change what is real. I'm sorry, sweetheart, but he's gone."

Rebel comes back and says, "Hawk, I'm heading out to get Ari. Do you need anything before I go?"

"Does Ari know?" Emma asks. Rebel shakes his head. "Who's gonna tell her?" she adds.

"I am," Rebel says sadly.

"Rebel, I have not seen Ari in a long time, but I think it would be better if I told her. We grew up together, and I believe she always looked up to me as a big sister."

Sometimes I forget that Emma has known Ice her entire life. Somehow, I think that the boy she knew as a kid is a lot different from the man he is now.

Hawk shakes his head. "Actually, Emma, she needs Rebel now." He turns back toward Rebel and says, "Reb, you go. Be careful and bring our girl back safe and sound."

"You got it, Hawk."

She interrupts him. "But Hawk ..."

I will give her one thing, she is definitely persistent.

"Emma, please. Don't interfere with club business. Trust me on this; I know what I'm doing. Ari and Reb are very close. He is who she will need. It's what Ice would have wanted."

A few minutes go by in silence. Annoyed, Emma says, "I need to go."

"Are you sure, sweetheart? You are still looking a little pale," Hawk replies. "You can stay here as long as you like."

"Thank you, Hawk, I really appreciate that. But I need to be alone for a while." She steps out of the van and begins to walk away. She turns back toward Hawk and asks weakly, "Are you really sure he is dead?"

Hawk looks confused by her question, and frankly so am I. Hawk says, "I am."

She comes back toward us and says, "Hawk, just hear me out for a minute." She looks around to make sure that it's just us, then says, "Caden didn't contact any of you after he left the clubhouse. So nobody has seen nor heard from him. Correct?"

"Yes," I reply. "As I said before, I am pretty sure I was the last person he spoke to in the club."

"Ok, so if nobody has heard from him and nobody has talked to him, what makes you both so sure he is dead? Maybe he has some grand plan to fix this. Maybe he is still with Mark. And, although I am stating the obvious here, let me add that you don't have his body."

Hawk looked over to me and says, "She's got a point." He turns back toward Emma and says, "I do still believe, however, that if he were alive he would've contacted us."

"I agree," she says. "But what if he can't? What if he is being held captive in the same place that Mark held me, only in a different room? I mean, think about this. If he had gone to rescue me, wouldn't he most likely go to where I was? I even yelled for him when I left in case he was there. I wanted him to know that Mark was letting me go. If he was planning any type of attack against Grayson, he would have waited until he knew I was safe."

"Well shit, Emma, I didn't think of any of that," Hawk replies. Shaking his head, he says, "You shame me. I should've thought this through more thoroughly."

"Well, you did have other things on your mind, like a blown-up clubhouse," she states sarcastically and then adds, "I think we should look for him first before we pronounce him dead. And I know where you can start."

We both look at her, surprised by her declaration. "How could you possibly know that?" Hawk asks.

"Because I have a pretty good idea where I was being held."

"So you know where Grayson was keeping you?" he asks hopefully. And for the first time since the explosion, I am hopeful as well.

"I don't know the exact address, but I have a good idea. I bet if we retraced my steps, I could find it again," Emma says encouragingly.

"What do you mean retrace your steps?" he asks.

"When Mark released me, he basically just kicked me out. I didn't have a car, and I had no idea where I was. So I started walking until I came across a gas station and used their phone to call a cab."

Looking hopeful, he says, "Look, Emma, I realize that you have been through a horrific ordeal, but you could really help us out a lot if you and I sit down somewhere and you tell me everything that has transpired over the last 48 hours."

She nods. "Yes, I will do what I can to help you."

"Thank you. I'm sure this will be difficult for you, but any information you can provide would help a lot." He pauses for a moment and then adds, "Why don't we get out of here? We'll go grab a cup of coffee and we can talk. I've been working on a new location for the club, but it will be weeks until it is ready. I've secured the vacant space above Betty's Dinor until we have something permanent. We can talk there."

"Ok, that sounds nice."

He turns back toward me. "Why don't you join us? I think having you there will help Emma." I glance over at Emma to make sure that she is good with that and she nods.

Hawk and I follow Emma on his bike. I love riding with him. He is so strong, and I feel safe when I wrap my arms around his waist. After all that's happened, I need a sense of security and Hawk definitely provides that.

CHAPTER 10

We get to the diner and take a seat in a booth in the back. The waitress comes to take our order and we all order coffee. Once she leaves, Hawk turns toward Emma and says, "Why don't you start from the beginning?"

"Ok, let me think for a minute." Emma takes a deep breath and then continues, "Rebel and I had just gotten back from the grocery store. No, wait—I need to go back a little further. At the grocery store, there was a man there with a devil tattoo on the back of his neck that seemed to be hovering around me. I actually bumped into him, and when Rebel came up and asked me what was wrong, the man was gone. I told Rebel about it, and when we left we saw a Harley in the parking lot. He asked me to watch the bike as we left to make sure it stayed parked. It did. When we got back to the house, we started to unload groceries."

Hawk interrupts her and asks, "Did anything look out of the ordinary when you got back to the house?"

"No, nothing that I noticed."

Looking disappointed, he says, "Ok, go on."

"So, Rebel was going into the house as I was coming out. I got to the car and started to grab a couple of bags, then everything went dark. The next thing I remember is being in a dark room, tied to a bed." She stops and I can see that she is getting uncomfortable.

Grayson must have done a number on her for her to hesitate like this.

Hawk senses it too and reaches for her arm. Laying his hand on her arm, he says, "Emma, I can only imagine what you have experienced during this ordeal. But, sweetheart, I really need to know everything. If we are ever going to find out what's happened to Ice, you need to tell me everything."

She nods and continues. "As I said, I woke up in a very dark room, naked and tied to a bed. Mark was there, and for the longest time, he would not speak to me. He only laughed. His laugh sounded as if it came from Satan himself. It terrified me, and I don't think I will ever forget it. I was really scared and the only thing that kept me sane was the hope that Caden or the club would find me. But nobody ever came."

"Emma, did Mark rape you?" Hawk asks the question that I wanted to ask her but couldn't.

Oh God, please say no.

She shakes her head. "No, he didn't. He tried, but when I refused to fight back it made him angry. So angry that he stopped and left the room."

"Oh thank God!" The words come out of my mouth before I can think. I am so relieved that he didn't, for her sake as well as for Ice's—if he is still alive.

"I'm thankful that he didn't rape you. You're gonna have enough scars from this ordeal to handle, you don't need any more on your plate," Hawk says. He then adds, "I assume the bruises on your face are from him?"

"Yes, he hit me in the face several times. I tried very hard to remain coherent, but it was difficult. I believe over the course of the time that I was there, which I am guessing was a little over 24 hours, that I went in and out of consciousness several times."

"Did he give you any reasons as to why he was doing this?"

"Yes," she replies. "He was very calculated in his reason, mentioning that he had Brianne worked over because she was threatening to tell me everything about him. He never went into details as to what that was, so I don't know what he didn't want me to know, but that he wanted to teach her a lesson." She stops as if she is trying to remember, then adds, "He also said that when I ran to Caden for help it only moved his plan along faster. When I asked him what plan, he said that he wanted to take back from Caden all that Caden took from him. None of that made any sense to me. I didn't have any clue what he was talking about—for all I knew, they had never met. I'm afraid that this was all my fault."

"Did he say anything else?" Hawk asks.

"He said that he was going to break me; that he was going to use me over and over again and then send me back to Caden and the club that rejected him. I didn't get the impression from him that he'd had Brianne killed, so I think she is still alive. If this is all my fault, Hawk, I'm so sorry."

Hawk asks, "Do you know what it was that he was trying to hide from you?"

Emma shakes her head and says, "No, I have no idea. He never said any more about it and when I asked he would just tell me to shut up."

Hawk then asks, "Can you remember anything else?"

"Yes, he said that he knew about my relationship with Caden longer than he had known me. I really didn't think about it much then, but looking back now, I find that very odd. Caden and I grew up together. How would Mark know anything about my childhood?"

"Not so odd, Emma. Based on what you have said, I think there is more to this than just a jealous boyfriend who lost his girl to the big bad biker. I believe there is a past connection between Ice and Mark that we don't know about. It could be the driving force for all of this. You and Brianne just got caught in the middle. So, please, stop blaming yourself. I believe we'll find out more once we get to where you were being held." He pauses briefly then adds, "Anything else?"

"He showed me a video that was recorded the other night."

"A video?" he asks.

"Yes, it was a video of a party at your clubhouse. Caden was with another woman. Mark said that he wanted me to see what kind of man I was involved with." She looks at me warily and adds, "I think it may have been you dressed up as me, but Mark never said anything to that effect. He just wanted me to think that Caden was cheating on me."

Suddenly I feel bad. She was never supposed to find out about that and I know it will break Ice's heart to know that she has. "It was me, but I was just a decoy, Emma. The club wanted the Satans to think that you were at the clubhouse. They didn't want them to know that Ice had sent you away. I promise, nothing happened."

"I know, Honey, but thanks for saying it. At first, I felt that Caden had abandoned me. I felt that I had nothing left and that if I got out alive, I still would have nothing 'cause I had lost Cade to another woman. I was praying that Mark would just get it over with, 'cause at that point, I was sure he was going to rape me and then kill me. I had given up. I think that is what saved me. I went completely still; I was lifeless and had stopped crying. I had no more fight in me. When I just laid there, silent, not even crying anymore, that's when Mark got angry and stormed out of the room. He left that video on and I watched it over and over. After viewing it several times, I realized that it was you with Caden." She glances over at me and shrugs. "Eventually I fell asleep or lost consciousness, I am not really sure which. When I came to, I heard talking out in the hallway, but the only voice I heard was Mark's. I realized he was talking to himself, but not just in the normal way people talk to themselves. No, Mark was actually arguing with himself. It was very creepy and I had never seen him do that before. He stormed into the room, still talking. He untied me and threw my clothes at me. He ordered me to get dressed and get out."

"That's it?" I ask, shocked that he would just let her go.

"Yeah, he basically just threw me out. That's why I had to find my way back home."

"So that is how you know where he kept you. Can you take us there?" Hawk says.

Emma nods. "Sure, I can try. I walked for several blocks until I found a gas station and called a cab from there. The clerk at the gas station gave me the address for the cab company. Wait, I think I still have it." She rummages through her purse and pulls out a slip of paper. "Here it is! The lady at the gas station gave me money for a cab to get home. I saved the address so that I could go back and repay her."

I do not understand this girl. Who does that?

"Wattsburg? What in the hell was he doing there?" Hawk is surprised—me too, for that matter. Wattsburg is a ways away from here. Why would he go so far?

She shakes her head. "I don't know. I remember when I left I looked back at the place that held so much horror for me and couldn't believe that it was a quaint little house in a residential neighborhood. It was kinda eerie, knowing what lived behind that door."

"Emma, are you up to going back to Wattsburg?"

"Absolutely!"

Emma and I follow Hawk back to his house, where he leaves his bike. Emma lets him drive the car and within forty-five minutes we're pulling into the parking lot of the gas station Emma spoke of. Hawk asks, "Do you remember how you got here?"

She gets out of the car and looks down all the possible streets we could go down and then she yells excitedly, "There! I came from that direction."

"Ok, let's go," Hawk says.

"Wait, let me do something first. I'll be real quick." She runs into the gas station.

"What in the hell is she doing?" Hawk asks.

I giggle in disbelief and say, "She's paying the clerk back."

"Damn woman," he replies shaking his head. Suddenly, I see Emma in a new light. After all the trauma that she has been through the last few days, Ice missing and having to go back and face the house that she was held captive in, she still makes a point to pay back the store clerk who helped her get home. I have to say, I'm impressed.

A few minutes later, she comes back out with the biggest smile on her face. Go figure. She gets in the car and proceeds to give Hawk directions. She's cautious and hesitant, making sure that she is leading us the right way. After we've travelled for several minutes, she says, "Drive slower, Hawk. We're almost there." Hawk slows down as instructed. Then Emma says, "That's the one. Right there, on the left. The one with the front porch and rocking chairs."

Hawk drives past it to the next block and parks the car. As he gets out of the car, he turns to us and says, "You both stay here for now until I check things out. I mean it, ladies! I don't need to be worrying about either of you right now. Stay put!" He reaches into his cut and pulls out a gun, turns the safety off, and cocks it. He turns and walks toward the house.

After Hawk leaves, Emma turns to me and says, "This is driving me crazy. How in the hell does he expect us to just wait here?"

"I know, I agree, but he's right, he doesn't need to be worrying about us too. Let's let him do what he needs to do and he'll come back for us."

I can tell she's not pleased, but she will have to get over it. Hawk is right, he doesn't need to worry about us. So we just sat there in an agonizing and awkward silence.

About fifteen minutes later, Hawk returns. He gets in and says, "I don't think anyone is there. I'm gonna call the boys for backup. We're going to go in." He calls Ryder to request backup and then turns to us and says, "You ladies coming?"

Neither of us hesitates and we jump out of the car. We walk back down the block to the house. When we get there, Hawk walks up on to the porch and rings the bell. He waits and when nobody answers he tries the door. It's locked. He goes around to the side and tries the side door. Surprisingly, it swings open. He turns back toward us and says, "Wait here." Hesitantly, he walks into the house, gun cocked and ready. He's gone for about five minutes and then comes back and says, "Come on."

We walk up the side porch steps and walk in the house. As soon as we get inside I can see that Emma isn't doing so well. She's nervous and on edge, understandably so. We continue through the mudroom and enter the kitchen. There is nothing unusual about the kitchen. Leaving the kitchen, we get to a long hallway with several closed doors. I shudder to think what is beyond those doors and suddenly I'm fearful of what we might find. I really don't think my heart will be able to take it if we find Ice in one of those rooms, dead. The first door reveals a small bathroom. Hawk opens the second door and we find that is a bedroom. Clothes are still hanging in the closet, but there's nothing out of the ordinary.

Hawk began to go through Mark's things on the dresser, opening dresser drawers and scoping out his closet.

On the other side of the hall, there are three closed doors. Hawk opens the first one and we see that it is an office, with several file cabinets and a desk. On the desk is a laptop. "I think we might find something here that will help us. When the boys get here, I will have Dbag check out the computer and the files," Hawk says as he leaves the room.

He then opens the next door and the stench is unbelievable. This has to be where he kept Emma. It is very dark and creepy. The walls are painted black, and with black curtains are drawn over the windows. There is a bed in the center of the room with ropes and chains attached all around it. Hanging on the wall are various whips, canes, and belts.

This fucker is crazy! I think to myself. *How the hell Emma could get mixed up with a psycho like this is beyond me. I wonder if she knew about all this or if this is a surprise to her.* By the horrified expression on her face, I'm guessing she had no clue.

I've never been one to have a filter and before I can stop myself I say, "Holy fuck, Emma! Is this the room that he held you in?"

Quietly, she replies, "Yes, I believe it is."

I can't help it. At that moment I feel so bad for her, I walk right over to her and hug her. "I'm so sorry."

"It's over now. We need to concentrate on finding Caden."

"What is that God-awful smell?" Hawk asks.

"Hell if I know," I reply, "but it smells like piss."

"I need to get out of this room. I'll have the boys go through shit in here when they get here," Hawk says and rushes from the room, Emma and I close behind him.

Hawk approaches the last door and opens it. From what I can see, it opens to a stairway that leads to the basement. "What the fuck!" Hawk yells.

I don't know what's wrong until the odor coming from below hits me. *Oh my God!* It is so bad that it overpowers the lingering smell from the last room. Hawk closes the door and walks into the kitchen. He comes back a few seconds later with three towels. He hands them to us, then opens the door again and we proceed down the stairs.

When we get to the bottom, Hawk flips the light switch. We all stand there in horror. What we see before us is more blood and gore than I can imagine from the worst murder scene. It looks like something out of the movie Frankenstein. There is a table in the middle of the room with all types of surgical instruments scattered on it, every one of them covered in blood. A stream of blood flows to the edge of the table and drips down to a puddle below. Whatever happened here was recent. The blood is not completely dried.

In the back, a body hangs from a hook on the rafters. It's dark and shadowed so I can't make out who it is. *Dear God, please don't let that be Ice,* I silently plead. Hawk approaches the body, looks at it and then asks Emma to come closer. She slowly walks over to him and I know she is thinking the same thing I am. When she gets up close, Hawk asks, "Is this Mark Grayson?"

"Yes." Simultaneously, we both breathe a sigh of relief.

Hawk shakes his head in disbelief, glances back to us and says, "Ice is back."

"Hawk, no, please say that Ice didn't do this," Emma pleads.

I've heard the stories, I've heard that he can be ruthless, but can he be so twisted as to do this to another human being? I've known Ice for a few years now and now that I think about it, I could see him doing this—especially if he is protecting someone he loves. And he loves Emma.

"It's his signature work. Grayson has been tortured, and flames have been carved into his chest. Ice did this, I'm sure of it," Hawk confirms.

"Fuck!" I reply.

Frantic, Emma asks, "What's going on? He's alive! Why aren't you both happy about this? Mark is dead and Cade is alive!" She pauses, waiting for us to say something, and when we don't she continues, "What's going on, you two? What aren't you telling me?"

"Emma, let's go back upstairs away from this mess and wait for the boys. Then I'll try to explain," Hawk replies.

We go back upstairs and sit down at the kitchen table. Hawk starts, "Emma, there are things about Ice that you don't know. I don't believe he is the same person that you grew up with." He hesitates for a moment, then continues, "Things have happened in his past that I believe have changed him."

"Hawk, I don't mean to be rude, but I know he's changed. I know he is not the boy that I knew as a child. But really, what does all that have to do with the dead psychopath in the basement?"

"I don't think you are understanding me. I'm trying to be delicate, but I see that's not working. So, I'm just gonna lay it out for you." He pauses for a moment, looking over at me for support. I know what he's about to tell her and frankly, I'm not so sure she can handle it. "Caden—no, not Caden ... Let me rephrase that. Ice is responsible for that bloodbath in the basement."

Emma shakes her head and yells, "No! No, Caden would never do that!"

"I know, you are right. Caden wouldn't have done that. But Ice would. He's done this before. I've seen this same type of handiwork before and Ice confirmed it himself that he did it."

"Are you trying to tell me that Caden—Ice, whoever—tortured Mark and murdered him?"

"Yes, that is exactly what I am telling you," Hawk replies.

"Why? Why would you think that?"

Before Hawk answers, we hear the roar of the Harley engines. The boys are here. When they come in, Hawk takes a minute to give them directions on what he wants to be done and then turns back toward Emma and says, "Where were we?"

"You were about to tell me why you think Caden is a cold-blooded killer," she states angrily. I do believe she is mad that he would make such an accusation. Well, I think our little sweet Emma is in for a rude awakening.

Hawk sighs and takes a deep breath and begins to tell Emma about the night Ace was killed.

When Hawk is done, Emma asks quietly, "That's why you call him Ice, isn't it?"

I knew the gist of what he had done, but I never knew all the details. So now I also know why they call him Ice.

Hawk nods. "Yes. It seems when those that he loves are hurt, something takes over in him and he turns cold. He becomes a predator that you don't want to mess with. You were threatened, and we all know how much he loves you. It only makes sense that he would react like that again."

"What happened after that?" she asks.

"After the massacre, we knew that the Satans would come looking for us. So, we voted to take down the Satans once and for all. We commissioned other Chapters in the area to assist. Anyone who refused was given the opportunity to leave or face punishment. Everyone stayed. I think after hearing what Ice had done, they not only respected him, they feared him. When people fear another person, it gives that person power over them and at times can be a bad thing. But in this situation, it worked to our advantage. The plan was easy, simple, and clean. We were going to blast the Satans straight back to hell. And that's exactly what we did. Unfortunately, it was only temporary, because as you and I both know, they came back."

"How did they come back?" she asks.

"Funny thing about revenge. As you know, it's fueled by emotion. When emotion is involved, common sense seems to hide in the back corners of your mind. We thought we had destroyed their club. But we didn't get them all. A few members survived, bided their time, and recruited new members. A few years later, they reemerged."

They talk for a few more minutes and then Ryder and Spike walk into the kitchen. Hawk discusses with them what they found and what they should take. He makes arrangements to get rid of Mark's body and then tells the boys to burn the house down.

Once he's done, Emma asks, "So, with this new discovery, do you think Caden is alive?"

Way to go Captain Obvious, of course he's alive.

Hawk hesitates for a moment, and then says, "Yes, darl'n, it's looking that way."

I was thinking the same thing. Now it's just a matter of time until he comes back. I'm not really sure how this will all play out or why he's staying away, but there is one thing I have learned about the man: he always has a reason.

Hawk explains to her that Ice is staying away for a reason and that we each have a part to play as the women who love him. It's kind of ironic: me playing the broken-hearted friend and Emma the grieving widow. I chuckle to myself.

We leave the house from hell. Emma drops Hawk and I back at his place so he can get his bike. After Emma leaves, I turn to Hawk and ask, "So you really think he's alive?"

He turns to me and smiles. "Yes, I do. How do you feel about that?" he asks.

"I'm thrilled, of course. We may not be together anymore, but that doesn't mean I don't care about what happens to him. And of course, I don't want him dead, Hawk. How could you ask such a thing?"

"Just trying to gauge where you're at. That's all." He gets on his bike and I climb on the back. As I'm putting on my helmet, he says, "I'm taking you to Betty's with me. I don't want to leave you here alone with all this shit that's going on. Ok?"

I nod, wrap my arms around him and he revs the engine and takes off. I've spent the last two nights at Hawk's house. He's got a great place and he's been the perfect gentleman. His spare bedroom has become mine for now. I guess it's a good thing, because I'm really not ready for another relationship right now and he is sure that I still have lingering feelings for Ice.

CHAPTER 11

When we get back to the diner, Hawk takes over the upstairs break room. I really don't have much to do so I just hang out in the corner playing on my phone, waiting for him to take me home.

After about an hour, his phone rings. He answers it and without any indication of who it is, he motions for me to leave the room. A few minutes later he comes out and says, "He's alive. Rebel has been talking to him. He wants you to stay at his lake house until we have a new clubhouse. Spike is on his way over to help you get your things and take me over there. Rebel will bring Ari to the house and then he will go get Emma. She will be staying there as well. Ice wants you three out of the way so he doesn't have to worry about the women he loves." His last words are laced with sarcasm. He's being very matter-of-fact and it is clear to me that he's not happy with the new arrangement, but he's going along with it because that's what his president wants.

"Oh, ok," I reply. I have to say, I'm a little disappointed that I won't be going back to Hawk's house. Still, I can't believe that after all these years, I'm finally going to see Ice's house.

Spike shows up with the SUV not long after Hawk calls him. We go back to Hawk's place to pick up the few personal things that I was able to salvage from the explosion and then we drive to the lake. The road that circles the lake is long and curvy. As we approach the back of the house, I'm amazed at the size. There is a two-car garage, even though I've never seen Ice drive anything except his Harley and the club SUV. Spike parks and we get out of the car and proceed to the door. As we walk around the house, I see that the front, which faces the lake, is all windows. The cedar and stone two-story house—more like mansion—is unbelievable. The house has three balconies with stone pillars going down to the main level. The entire right corner of the house is all windows and I can only imagine the view from the inside. Toward the center of the house is the main balcony, and by looking in the windows I can see that it opens into a huge great room that spans the entire height of the house. To the right of the house is a stone walkway that leads to a breezeway underneath the balconies that lead to the door. *Holy fuck.*

The inside is even more amazing. There is a large great room that encompasses the downstairs, with vaulted ceilings, a huge kitchen with a bar off to the right, and a game room with a pool table to the left of the kitchen. It's fucking unbelievable. I always figured that Ice had money, but never in a million years did I expect his home to be like this. And here I was worried about there not being enough room for us.

Ari is sitting at the bar when I walk in and she smiles brightly. I've only seen her a few times when she makes her way to the club parties on the weekends, but every time I see her she always gives me a warm smile.

"Hey, Ari," I say. "It's good to see you, sweetie."

"Hey, Honey. Can you believe this mess?" she says.

I can't help but laugh. "It's a mess alright," I reply.

"There are two extra rooms upstairs, next to my room. I think Rebel claimed one and the other one is for you."

"Where's Emma gonna sleep?" I ask.

"Oh, she's got Cade's room, on the third floor."

I know she didn't mean to dig the knife in, but fuck, sometimes it still hurts. "Oh yeah. I didn't think of that. So Emma is here?"

"Yeah, she's upstairs." She turns to me and says, "You know, it's been years since I've seen Emma." She pauses and then adds, "I used to hate her. She spent all her time with Caden and he never spent time with me. I was so jealous of her."

Oh, sweetheart, I know exactly how you feel. I really thought I was over all this. I know that Ice is not the guy for me, so I really don't understand all this animosity I feel towards Emma right now. Hawk must have sensed it too, now that I think about it— that must be why he was so angry earlier.

I turn back toward Ari and say, "I'm just gonna drop my stuff off upstairs and then I'll be down. Are you hungry?" I ask her.

"Yeah, we were hoping you would whip up something," she says and goes back to playing some game on her phone.

"I'm pretty sure I can handle that," I say as I proceed up the stairs. When I get to the second floor, I look up to the next flight. I can see the light on and a sudden melancholy feeling washes over me. Maybe I'm just feeling this way because I've been so worried about Ice...perhaps I just need to see him. Maybe once I see him, I will go back to my being ok with all this. Taking the room that obviously was not claimed, I drop my things on the bed and make my way downstairs.

Ari is still at the table and I head straight for the kitchen and quickly get to work. I go through the cabinets, refrigerator, and freezer to see what is available to me. There isn't much, but it looks like someone went and picked up some groceries. There's milk, cream, butter, lettuce, and asparagus, plus all the essentials in the refrigerator. In the freezer, I find chicken breasts and some ground beef. It's not a lot to work with, but I pull the chicken out and place it in the microwave to defrost.

"Hey, Ari," I call out.

"Yeah, Honey?" she replies.

"Got any white wine, hun?" I ask.

"Sure, I'll get it." A few seconds later she comes in with three bottles of white wine. "I've got pinot grigio, chardonnay, or sauvignon blanc."

"The chardonnay would be perfect." She sets it on the counter and takes the others back.

A little while later Emma comes downstairs.

"Hey, Honey. That smells amazing. Whatcha making?" Emma asks.

"Hey, Emma. Chicken Marsala—you smell the wine. It makes the whole meal."

"I wasn't hungry, but now that I smell that, suddenly I'm starved. You are a fantastic cook."

"Thank you. I don't know about being fantastic, but I do enjoy it." I pause and then add, "So what do you think about all this? It's like a slumber party of some sort." I chuckle and say, "I'm too old for slumber parties."

She laughs too. "Aren't we all? But I look at it this way: Cade is doing everything he can to keep the ones he loves most safe. I'm just thankful that he is still alive."

"Yeah, me too."

Ari comes back in and she sits with Emma, watching me work. They offer to help several times, but I do much better in the kitchen on my own. But I have to say, I'm loving the company.

"Honey, why are you making so much?" Emma asks.

"I need to feed the boys, too."

"Boys?"

"Yeah, Hawk, Spike, and Rebel stayed. Once they heard I was cooking, they weren't leaving. I think they are already sick of eating at the diner." I laugh. "They are out back sitting by the lake. I think Rebel is going to stay with us, just in case."

"Just in case?" she asks.

"Yeah, they want to make sure one of the guys is with us at all times. No worries, they are just looking out for our safety," I say, trying to reassure her.

"Oh. I see. Do you really think we are in danger?"

Ari chimes in and says, "If my brother believes we are, then we are. His instincts are right on, and I would never question something that he feels in his gut."

I nod in agreement. "She's got that right."

After dinner, we spend the remainder of the night chatting. Hawk and Spike leave not long after we finish with the dinner dishes and as I expected, Rebel stays behind. He's pretty much keeping to himself, just hanging out on the recliner. His phone rings and he answers it, speaking in hushed tones. I wonder what's up with that, but I don't question him.

It's been a long day and we decide to call it a night. As we get up to head to our respective bedrooms, Emma asks Rebel, "Aren't you going to bed?"

"Naw, not yet. I got a couple of things to do first. Don't worry about me, Emma dear. It's all good. Sweet dreams, ladies," he says and Ari and I proceed up the stairs.

"Ok, if you say so. Goodnight, Rebel," Emma replies as she follows Ari and me up the stairs.

CHAPTER 12

I wake feeling refreshed and I realize that this is the first time since all this happened that I have actually slept. I never thought about it much until recently, but Ice isn't just the club's president; he also serves another purpose. He grounds everyone. Knowing that he is at the helm making sure everyone is safe is comforting. When we thought he was gone, I think we were all just going through the motions.

Speaking of motions, I make my way to the bathroom. Even though I feel rested, I look awful. I pick up a brush and brush my hair and then I just stare at myself in the mirror. *Oh, fuck it. I need coffee.* I give up and make my way downstairs. I don't even bother changing, I am sure my t-shirt and leggings are appropriate attire in mixed company. And if not, then screw them. I'm comfortable.

I walk into the kitchen and find Rebel and Emma sitting at the table. Rebel looks at his watch, points at it and says to Emma, "See? Like clockwork." They laugh.

Why do I feel that I have been the butt of a bad joke? "You two are chipper this morning," I say, irritated. I'm not a morning person and I hate being laughed at, especially before I've had my coffee.

"Yes, we are. You might want to get yourself some coffee and maybe you could join us," Rebel says sarcastically.

"Fuck you, Rebel!" *Oh, this is gonna be a fun morning.*

We spend the remainder of the day just hanging around the house. We're not allowed to leave, but the guys come and go. Rebel is with us all day and when his cell rings, he steps outside. *What the hell? We're part of this now, can't they see that?* A few minutes later he comes back in and says, "Hey, girls. I just got off the phone with Hawk. Ice's memorial will be held next Friday."

"Rebel, that's over a week away. Why are we waiting so long?" I say.

"We got a lot of members coming from all over; they need travel time. Hawk decided to give them that time, and since he's the new prez in the eyes of the outside world, we do what he tells us to do."

I smirk and roll my eyes. He continues, "So, as I was saying, the memorial will be held next Friday. We are securing a location at Kandi's to accommodate the members from out of town that will be coming in, as well as using it for a clubhouse until the new one is fitted to meet our needs." He looks over at me and says, "Honey, you will be in charge of coordinating logistics for our guests. Emma, you and Ari can help with that. Honey has a lot of experience handling this, you both can learn a lot from her." The girls nod and look at Rebel, waiting for him to say more. "What?" he asks.

"Well, what do we do between now and next Friday?" Emma asks.

For a minute, he looks at them as if he is talking to three airheads. Then he says, "As I said, you and Ari will be helping Honey with logistics."

I totally get why Emma asked that question. She has no idea what is involved in getting ready for something like this. She can't even begin to fathom the number of clubs that will show up for Ice. I step in and try to explain. "Emma, dear, what Rebel is saying is that there is going to be a lot of out-of-towners coming in over the next few days. We will work together to ensure that everyone has a place to sleep, that they are fed, and that everyone is comfortable."

"Oh," Emma says as if she understands.

Rebel shakes his head in disbelief. He just doesn't get it. "Is everyone staying here?" Emma asks.

"No, they will be staying at Kandi's. Which means that we will need to gather up blankets and pillows and get some food. It's gonna be a week, and we better get started," I reply.

"Isn't Kandi's that strip club?" Emma asks.

Ok, now she is getting on my nerves. How many times do we have to explain this to her? "It is, but there are rooms in the back that we can use. I'm surprised Hawk didn't think of it before, it's perfect as an interim clubhouse," I reply curtly.

"Ok, just let me know what you need me to do," Emma says.

Finally. "Well, first, why don't you and I sit down and figure out food? Then we can send Ari with Rebel to do some grocery shopping and get it all delivered to Kandi's. Then, you and I can get on the phone with the other old ladies to secure the other items we need. Sound good?"

"Sounds good," Emma replies.

"Yep, sounds good to me," Ari chimes in.

We sit down at the bar and work on planning food and all the other things that we need to get together, making lists and taking notes. This takes up most of the day. While we were taking care of logistics, Tiny brought the pick-up so Rebel can take Ari grocery shopping. After they leave, I notice Emma fading. It seems as if she is off in another world or something.

I stare at her curiously when she looks up at me and says, "Honey, what else do you need me to do?"

"You're back with us," I say and smile.

"What do you mean? I've been sitting here the entire time," she says as she yawns.

"Sweetheart, your body may have been here, but your head was a million miles away."

"Oh, that. I just have a lot on my mind. Things that I need to deal with."

I really do feel bad for her. She's been through a lot. I get up from the chair and give her a hug. "If you need to talk, I'm here, sweetie. You've been through a lot the last couple of weeks. Nobody can blame you if you are still dealing with the ramifications of all that."

"Thanks, Honey. I really appreciate it and in time, I may just take you up on it." She pauses and then adds, "Can I tell you something?"

"Sure, hon."

"I was so jealous of you when I first got back in touch with Caden. I knew I came between you two. I felt bad to an extent but was more jealous than anything else. You know the man that he is today, and all I had was the boy I had known 20 years ago." She looks away briefly and then back at me. I know she is waiting for me to say something, but how do I respond to that? So instead I remain quiet and let her continue. "And, well, now that I have gotten to know you, I really like you. You've become a good friend to me."

I smile and say, "Well, that makes us even. I was jealous of you, too." *Sometimes, I still am.* "I knew that you and Ice had a history and I guessed that you were the reason he never settled down with anyone. He was never going to make me his old lady. I never realized that, however, until you came."

"I'm sorry." There is an awkward silence between us and then she adds, "I really never meant to hurt anyone by coming back into his life."

"I know that, really I do. I was hurt at first, but I know that you are the one that has been meant for him all along. I've never seen him content, truly content, like he is with you. I loved him—hell, I think I still do in a way. But it really makes me happy to see him happy. That's what's important."

"And what about you?"

"Oh, now don't you go worrying about me. I know there's someone out there for me. There has to be, right?" I ask with a laugh.

"I know there is!" She beams. "What will you do now? Will you stay with the club?"

"Ice has assured me that I will always have a place with the club. He has told me over and over again that this club is my home. So, I plan on sticking around. Besides, I really enjoy taking care of these boys and I do consider you a friend." I let the silence between us settle and then say, "You know, he took me in when I had nothing. I will never forget what Ice and this club have done for me."

"What happened to you before you came to the club?" Emma asks.

"That, my dear Emma, is a story for another day. Right now, we have work to do." Emma is definitely growing on me, but I'm not ready to tell her my sad tale.

"Can I ask another question?" she asks.

"Sure, hon."

"Is Honey your real name?" I laugh. Of all the questions she could ask, that was not what I was expecting.

"No, it's Amanda." I don't have the heart to tell her that Ice gave me the nickname, so I lie and say, "The boys gave me the name "Honey" and it kinda stuck." I pause and look at her oddly and say, "Did I really just say that?" And we both start laughing.

Just then, Hawk walks through the front door. "Hey, girls. How are things going here?" Emma looks from Hawk to me and then back at Hawk again.

I look at her incredulously.

"What?" she asks.

"What's going on in the head of yours, Emma?" I give her a look that says, *I know you're up to something.*

"Not a thing," she replies smugly. "Don't you need to tell Hawk about all the arrangements we've made today?"

I proceed to go over everything with Hawk. He seems pleased with the progress Emma and I made today.

A couple of hours later, Rebel and Ari return and inform us that everything has been dropped at Kandi's and that they picked up some things for us here at the house as well. Rebel and Ari go out to carry them in and when they are gone, Emma asks a lot of questions. She seems especially curious about Rebel and Ari. I think she is playing matchmaker. But I also think she is right. I know that Rebel has had a thing for Ari, but I don't think he's said anything to Ice about it. Frankly, I'm not sure how Ice will take it. He's very protective of his kid sister and rightly so.

"Rebel has been dancing around his feelings for her for as long as I can remember. He's worried that Ice will beat the shit out of him if he messes with his sister. I can't say I really blame him, but at least he could ask him. Don't ya think?"

"He should ask him. What could it hurt?" Emma says.

"For most people, it couldn't. But if Ice is totally against the idea, he could get so pissed off that Rebel would even think about dating his kid sister that he'd beat the shit out of him. And Ice would win. That's why Rebel is scared."

"Would he really hurt him, just for that?" she asks curiously.

"Hell yeah, he would. That's almost as bad as one of the guys going after his old lady," I say as Rebel and Ari come back in carrying a few bags.

As we start to empty the bags that have been placed on the counter, Ari comes up behind us, drops her bags on the counter, and runs upstairs to her room. We then hear the door slam. Rebel goes out the front door and slams that door too. Emma looks over at me and I just roll my eyes, silently telling her to just leave it alone.

Several minutes later, they come back into the kitchen. "You two finally kiss and make up?" I ask in my best motherly tone.

Rebel gives me a look that says, *Let it go, Honey.* Out loud he replies, "Yeah, we're all good here."

"Yep, all good," Ari adds.

CHAPTER 13

We spend the remainder of the week preparing food that we can freeze and store at Kandi's. The out-of-town guests are arriving daily and Rebel and Hawk have been so busy, we've hardly seen them during the day. They always come for dinner, and Rebel always stays, but that's about it.

The service is today and frankly, even though I know that Ice is alive, it's the last thing I want to attend. But I do, and other than the Satans showing up, everything goes without a hitch. They didn't cause any problems, but they made damn sure that their presence was known.

Rebel, Ari, and Emma left the after-party early, but Hawk, being the acting prez, had to stay. When we get back to the house, all hell breaks loose. Hawk sees Rebel come out of Ari's room and I can see his anger rise. "What?" Rebel asks defensively.

"Isn't that Ari's room you just walked out of?" he asks smugly.

"Fuck you, Hawk. She fell asleep on the couch. I carried her to bed. End of story. Get your fuckin' mind out of the gutter."

"Yeah, right. Wait until Ice finds out you have been banging his sister."

Rebel gets in Hawk's face and says, "Look, motherfucker. You're talking about stuff you know nothing about. Until you get your facts straight, I suggest you keep your fuckin' mouth shut. You got me?"

Hawk pushes him away and says, "You better remember who you are talking to."

"Fuck you! I don't give a fuck who you are, and neither will Ice—especially if he hears you talking shit about his kid sister."

I've had enough, so I step between them and say, "Boys, enough! Hawk, get yourself a beer and cool off. Rebel, you pour yourself a drink, too. You are both acting like a couple of ten-year-olds. Enough is enough! Ice would be pissed at you both, hearing you talk like this." I look over at Rebel and say, "Grow up, Rebel!" Then I turn to Hawk and say, "And you! Go get laid and unwind. You have been wound tighter than a fucking top recently." I scowl at them both. They know better; we don't need this shit right now. "If you two don't straighten up, I'll put you both over my knee. And don't think I can't do it!" I stomp off and head to my room. *Damn fucking alpha bikers. I swear their egos are bigger than their Harleys.*

The next several days fly by. Everyone else still believes that Ice is dead and we haven't seen or heard from him. Well, us girls, that is. I'm sure the boys have. But we don't see them much, as they are in constant meetings. That leaves Emma, Ari, and me to entertain ourselves. When Rebel can't be at the house, he makes sure that one of the prospects is there to babysit us. Usually, it's Tiny. We actually ask for him. He's great to have around, as he goes out of his way to keep us entertained. He plays board games and cards with us and one of us girls always beats him. But I think he lets us win. And he is quite funny.

But when Tiny isn't around, it gets downright boring. Emma, Ari and I have gotten really close and I like that. I don't have many girlfriends and the ones that I do have I don't see very often. Obviously, Emma and Ari aren't going anywhere, so I'm hopeful. I still have bouts when I can't help feeling jealous of Emma, and sometimes even Ari. They are both a part of Ice's life and sometimes I feel like the outsider. But then they do something really sweet and I feel like I do belong.

It does get better, but we all are just patiently waiting for Ice to come home.

Tonight, I decide to go and find something for dinner in the freezer downstairs. Ari is taking a nap and Emma is reading. I come up from the basement and find Hawk and Ryder in the family room talking to Emma.

"Hey guys," I say. Hawk looks up and smiles at me. I blush slightly; his adoration sometimes makes me uncomfortable. But before I can say anything, I am pulled into a great big bear hug.

"Hey, Honey girl! I've missed you!" Ryder says.

"I've missed you too, big guy!" I say, smiling. I see Hawk watching us out of the corner of my eye and he looks pissed. He gets so damn jealous and we aren't even officially together, yet. I can't deal with that kind of possessiveness. If he really wants a relationship with me, he had best get over it.

We hear the hum of a Harley pulling in the driveway and I soon realize that it's not just a Harley. That's Ice. I can tell that Hawk and Ryder already know that it's him, but Emma is confused. She gets up from the couch and walks over to the window. I watch as her curious expression turns to excitement when she realizes that he's home. Everything in me wants to run out there and hug him and welcome him home, but I know I can't. I stand firm as best I can.

"Hey guys, Ice is home!" Emma screams and runs to the door. Just then the door opens and she literally jumps in his arms. I watch him hold her tight and wait for them to finish their reunion.

Then I casually walk over to him. He releases Emma and turns to me and says, "Hey, sweetheart."

He holds out his arms and just like it is the most natural thing, I walk into them. *Why does this feel so right?*

He says, "I told you I'd be back."

"Yes, you did! But I have to say, even though we knew you were alive, I found it hard to believe until I actually saw you!" I reply. There is tension in the room and I realize that perhaps I overstepped. To lighten the mood, I take my right hand and hit him hard on the arm. "Don't you ever scare me like that again!" I scold.

"Yes, ma'am," Caden replies. "Is dinner ready yet? I'm starved," he adds.

"Not yet, but I'll get working on it right away," I reply. Just as I turn to go back toward the kitchen I see the look on Emma's face. She can fucking see right through me and suddenly I'm embarrassed. She has got to know that he will never have the same feelings for me that he has for her. He would never cheat on her. And I know, in time, I will no longer struggle with my feelings for him. It's only been a couple of weeks and already it's getting better. But fuck. I thought he was dead, then I was told that he was alive, but I haven't seen him since he left me the day the clubhouse blew up...what does she expect? Of course I'm a mess of mixed-up emotions.

We are all talking and carrying on when Ari comes downstairs. She says, "What is going on out here? You guys make more noise than the sex-crazed women at a Maroon 5 concert!" We stop talking and look at her. When she realizes that Ice is home, she screams and runs into his arms. "Caden! You're home!"

"Hey, doll face! How's my best girl?" I love to watch him and Ari interact. He is such a great brother to her and I still revel in the fact that he has raised her since she was twelve. Ice is still talking with Ari when I see Emma hold her hand in front of her mouth and run from the room and up the stairs. Just as I'm about to follow her to make sure she's ok, Ice walks by me and says, "I got this Honey, thanks." I nod and step aside so that he can continue up the steps.

A few minutes later, Ice and Emma come back down. I look at her closely and I know. She has a glow about her—and combined with the sudden sickness, it can only be one thing. I watch her pick at her food throughout dinner and when she excuses herself and says that she is still not feeling well, I know my assumptions are correct. Emma is pregnant.

As soon as I realize that, the memories begin coming back. I fight to keep them at bay. *No. No. No. Please God, I can't think about that now!* I plead with my brain, but it doesn't work.

I've been in New York now for almost a month and I know that I am pregnant. I've been experiencing all the symptoms for the last couple of weeks and yesterday the doctor confirmed my worst fear. This can't be happening to me...but it is. There is no question as to what I plan to do. The abortion is scheduled for tomorrow.

My heart begins to ache as I remember that awful day.

I arrive at the doctor's office and they begin the procedure. They are doing a medical abortion, not surgical, and I am thankful for that. First they have to perform a sonogram to determine that the pregnancy is viable, which it is. Now they can proceed. They give me a methotrexate injection, and the minute it goes into my arm, I feel as if I am on death row getting a lethal injection. I guess that's really what this is, but unfortunately it doesn't kill me, just my unborn child. They send me home with some antibiotics. I really don't feel any different, other than the fact that there is nothing left of my heart.

I can't stop the tears that are now falling down my cheeks.

I go back five days later to get the next lethal dose. They give me miso-something, but they also refer to it as MTX. It's an odd name for something so deadly. They tell me that this will trigger contractions and that they could happen within a few hours or several days. I pray that it only takes a few hours and for once in my life, God answers my prayers. Three hours later the contractions begin. I know my baby is already dead. I can't stop crying. I feel dead inside. Once the fetus—I can't call it a baby anymore—is expelled, I'm sent home with more antibiotics. I have to come back in seven days for a final exam.

I fucking hate it when I get so emotional. It was just an injection and some pills and my child was gone. But it was the worst two weeks of my life and I still suffer from the emotional damage of what I had done.

How can a simple procedure be so life-altering?

CHAPTER 14

The next morning, I'm downstairs getting coffee when Ice comes down. I look up and smile and ask, "How's Emma feeling?"

He shakes his head. "Not so good. I expect her to stay in bed most of the day. I told her if she isn't better tomorrow, she's going to the doctor."

He looks really worried. I want to tell him what I think—no, not what I think, what I know—but it's not my place.

I try to picture him as a father. I think about how he has raised his sister, how strong he is for everyone he's responsible for. Even though he's done some questionable things, I think he is a good man. He will make a fantastic father. Suddenly a thought strikes me: I never thought about Ice as the father of my kid. Isn't that normal when you fall in love with someone, you try to picture them as your husband, your kid's father, etc? I never did that. Curious.

"I'll make a batch of chicken soup. Maybe that will help settle her stomach," I say.

"Thanks, dear. Keep an eye on her for me, will ya?" he asks and then turns toward Rebel. "We need to head out soon."

"What for?" Rebel asks.

"'Cause we have shit to do."

"Like what?"

"First of all, we need to call church. We need to get moving on the new clubhouse and move forward with the gun trade. Is that ok with you?" Ice has that sarcastic tone in his voice and Rebel immediately gets it.

"Hey man, I didn't mean ..."

Ice is clearly pissed, and he cuts Rebel off. "Then don't fucking ask 'like what?' when I say we have shit to do!"

That's one thing I have learned over the years, do your best never to piss Ice off. Being on his shit list is not a good place to be.

"Yes, sir!" Rebel replies.

Ice's phone rings and he and Rebel step out of the kitchen as he takes the call. About twenty minutes later, Ice comes back into the kitchen.

"Would you like some breakfast?" I ask him.

I get another one of his panty-dropping smiles and he replies, "Naw, darl'n, I'm good."

I get up from the table and pour myself another cup of coffee. When I turn around, he's gone. *Oh well, he must have been in a hurry.* I take a sip of my coffee and then decide I need to get started on the soup.

Several hours later, Emma walks into the kitchen. I say, "Well, there is our little sleepyhead. How are you feeling, hun?"

"A little better. Have I been sleeping all day?" she asks, confused.

"You have. Whatever bug you got, it has totally wiped you out. I made you some chicken soup. Are ya hungry?"

"I'm sorry, Honey, but I don't think I can eat anything right now. But I would love some ginger ale if we have some."

"We don't, darl'n, but let me shoot a text to Ice to pick some up for you. The boys are on their way back. He texted a few minutes ago to let me know that Hawk would be joining us for dinner." I pull out my phone and send the text.

"Can I help you with anything?" she asks.

"No way, baby doll, you are not well. You just sit your pretty little self down and relax. I got this." I pause and then add, "And just so you know, Ice gave me strict orders: if you are not better by tomorrow, you are going to the doctor."

"Yeah, he told me," she says, defeated.

A little over an hour later, the boys return. Rebel gets back first, Ice and Hawk come in not long after. Ice greets Emma and then goes into the kitchen to get her a glass of ginger ale and takes it back out to her.

When dinner is ready we all sit down to eat. I notice that Emma still isn't eating. "Do we happen to have any saltines?" she asks.

"We sure do," I reply. I rummage through one of the cabinets and produce a box of crackers and put them on the table in front of her. The saltines will help settle her stomach, especially if she is experiencing morning sickness. Suddenly I feel like a mother bear and want to protect her. I swear these changing emotions are driving me crazy. I wish I could control them. I wish the jealousy wouldn't creep its way in, but luckily right now, it's gone. I'm pleased when I see that she has eaten all her soup.

After dinner, everyone goes into the family room to hang out and visit. I stay in the kitchen and clean up. Emma and Ari insist on helping, but I shoo them both away. I need some me time. Cleaning is therapy for me. The time alone will give me the opportunity to sort through all these conflicting emotions that I am having.

Several minutes after everyone leaves the kitchen, Hawk comes back in.

"Hey Honey," he says.

"Hey," I reply. *Well, so much for me time.*

"Can we talk for a minute?" he asks.

"Sure, what's up?" I reply. I know exactly what he wants to talk about and I'm not sure that I am ready to have this conversation.

"I wanted to see how you were doing."

"I'm doing fine, Hawk. Really," I reply.

"Have you thought any more about us?" he asks.

"Yeah, I have."

"Yeah?"

I'm tired of the beating around the bush on this. Maybe if I just give in to the feelings that I have for Hawk, I can move on and get over the mixed emotions I have about Ice.

I walk over to Hawk. Standing close, I wrap my arms around him and pull him close. He looks a little surprised by my boldness and before he can speak I move in and kiss him. He hesitates at first, not sure what to make of it, and then all his inhibitions subside when he pulls me to him and takes over the kiss, drinking from my lips. It's nice. My body goes weak and I know I made the right decision. Hawk has been nothing but good to me. He's been my confidant, my friend, and the only one whom I can confide in and I know he will still love me. He's always been there for me and I've taken him for granted for far too long.

When the kiss breaks, he says breathlessly, "I've waited so long for you, Amanda."

"I know, you've been so patient with me. I'm sorry that it took me so long to take a chance on us."

"Can I take you to dinner Saturday?"

"I'd love that." I couldn't make the smile on my face go away if I wanted to. I'm too happy to care.

"I'm gonna make you so happy, babe," Hawk says as he pulls me into a bear hug.

When he releases me, I say, "I know."

He steps away and says, "I gotta go. See you tomorrow?"

"Count on it," I reply and with that, he turns to leave.

CHAPTER 15

The next day, the boys leave early for a meeting. Emma has a doctor's appointment. Ari and I offer to go with her, but she insists that she wants to go alone. It's a pretty quiet day until everyone comes back. When Emma gets back from the doctor's, she goes straight to her room. I don't question her because I figure she is still not feeling well and just wants to rest.

When the boys come back, dinner is almost ready. Rebel's phone rings just as they walk in the door and her steps into the living room to take it. Ice goes upstairs to check on Emma and when they come back down, Emma is practically glowing. Ice looks a bit wary and I realize my assumptions are correct. They're having a baby. He then confirms my suspicions with the big announcement. My heart shatters, not only for my unborn child, but for the fact that it's not me having Ice's baby. *Why couldn't it have been me? I would have done anything for him.* I laugh at myself. I still would do anything for him.

"OMG!" Ari squeals. "I'm gonna be an aunt!" She runs over to Emma and hugs her tightly then steps back. "Are you really pregnant?" I laugh at her excitement. Despite my jealousy, I have to say that I am excited for them as well.

Emma laughs too. "Yes, Ari, I'm really pregnant, and yes, you are gonna be an aunt."

She runs over to Ice and jumps up and down. "My big brother is gonna be a daddy! I'm so excited!" she sings.

I walk over to Emma and give her a hug. I'm fighting back tears and I don't know if they are tears of joy for them or tears of loss for me—not for Ice, but for the baby I lost all those years ago. I will regret that every day of my life. Ice is the only one that knows about that and I prefer to keep it that way. He catches my solemn look and I know he's thinking about it. I smile at him to show him that I am truly happy for him and Emma. He replies silently, indicating to me that he understands just by the look on his face. I walk over to him and say awkwardly, "You're gonna make one hell of a dad, Ice."

"Ya think?"

"Hell yeah, I sure do," I say confidently.

He smiles and then replies with feeling, "Thanks, Honey, that means a lot."

He looks around at everyone and smiles. "Well, this could not have come at a better time. We are all whole, we've finally made peace with the Satans, and things should be calming down now significantly."

Before anything else is said, we hear Rebel yell, "What the fuck! What do you mean you don't know where they are?" Ice turns to Rebel to see what's going on.

"Find them! I'll get there as soon as I can!" He hits end on his conversation and looks at Ice with total despair in his eyes. I've never seen Rebel like this. Rebel says, "Ice, man, I need you. We have to go to Belfast."

"Belfast? What the fuck, Rebel? I just fucking got home and you're telling me I have to leave. Have you lost your mind, brother?"

"That call was from my brother, Damon. My parents are missing. Actually, they've been missing for a couple of weeks now, but those fuckers decided to wait until now to tell me," Rebel replies.

"Missing?" Ice asks. Rebel goes on to explain that his parents are IRA and something went down in Ireland and he needs to go there and find them. Ice doesn't even hesitate. He just got back with his family, but instead of saying no and telling Rebel he's on his own, he readily agrees to help him.

Emma, Ari, and I are not too pleased about this as we soon realize that our men are going to Ireland. It's not gonna be a vacation, either, as we gather there is quite a bit of danger involved. And most importantly, they are not taking us along.

They spend the next day engrossed in making plans. We hardly see them, but I am pleased to find out that Hawk is not going. Ice needs him to stay back and move things forward with the MC. I have to say that I kind of like those plans. This change in our relationship status is new and the thought of him leaving indefinitely had me worried. I also think it will be good for us that the Ice factor will be thousands of miles away.

The boys are leaving tomorrow morning and we are having a 'going away' dinner for them tonight. Ari is heading back to school tomorrow as well. It will be just Emma and me here. She and Ice have assured me that I can stay as long as I want until the new clubhouse is finished. Everything seems to be settling down, except for the guys leaving. But I know they will be ok, they will do what they have to do and be back before we know it.

I'm in the kitchen working on dinner when Emma comes in. "Hey girl," I say as she walks in.

"Hey. Can I help you with anything?"

I smile and reply, "No love, I'm good. But thanks for asking." I'm in an unusually good mood today and I begin to hum. I catch Emma watching me curiously and I know she is wondering what's up. Finally, she asks, "Ok, Honey, what's going on?"

I stop humming and look up at her. "Nothing,"

"Don't tell me 'nothing', girl. You're humming! You never hum!" she says and she's fucking right. I can't help but laugh.

"Am I that transparent?"

"Yeah! So what's up?"

"Do you really want to know?"

"I wouldn't have asked if I didn't want to know. Silly girl, you've become a good friend. If something is going on with you, of course I want to know."

"Well, I think things might be getting better for me in the relationship department," I say and I can't help the smile on my face. Hell, every time I think of that kiss I smile.

"Oh my God! Did Hawk finally admit that he has feelings for you?"

"How did you know?" I pause then say, "I mean, what makes you think Hawk has feelings for me?"

"Oh come on, really? That man is so smitten with you it's written all over his face. I've been waiting for him to make his move. I'm guessing that he finally did?"

"Well, he didn't really come out and say he had feelings for me, but he did invite me out to dinner on Saturday."

"Really?"

"Really."

"It's about damn time! I'm so excited for you!" Emma squeals. Hesitantly, she adds, "You did say you'd go, didn't you?"

I laugh. "Of course I did! I may be foolish sometimes, but I'm not a fool." Suddenly, I feel that I need to reassure her about my feelings for Ice. There are times when she looks at me and I can see her questioning my feelings for him.

"Can I tell you something? When the club first took me in, it was Hawk who was always there for me. He and I became close and I always hoped that there would be more than friendship between us. But it never happened. When Ice started to take an interest in me, I had pretty much given up on Hawk," I lie. The last thing I want her to know is how deep my feelings for Ice run. Yeah, I know he will never be mine, but she doesn't need to know exactly how I feel about him.

I continue, "I knew that if I started a relationship with Ice, Hawk would back off. These boys don't mess with another brother's woman. I mentioned to Hawk one night that Ice had expressed an interest in me and he told me to go for it." I shrug. "I took that as him saying that he didn't want me. Looking back now, and knowing more about the club and the loyalty between the brothers, I realize that he was just stepping down for his prez."

"So, it was Hawk that you wanted all along?" she asks, and I can hear the hopeful tone in her voice. Even though everything I just said to her is a lie, it's what she needs to hear.

"At the time, yes. But as you know, I did fall in love with Ice." She knows that I loved him, so I can't lie here. "When Ice and I started dating, if that is what you want to call it, Hawk backed off completely. I even lost the friendship that we had built. Then you came into the picture."

"I'm sorry."

"Oh, Emma, don't be. At first, as you know, I was hurt and very jealous of you. But as time moved on and you and I became friends, I realized that it was always Hawk that I had wanted. During those early months, he and I developed a bond. I've always loved him, deeper than I could love any other man. I am really looking forward to our date next week." I think I've finally given her the reassurances that she wants. I care for Hawk, I really do, but I'm not in love with him. At least not yet, but I hope that our relationship will develop into something special.

"I think the feeling is mutual. I really do. I have watched him with you and it is so obvious. He chooses your company over anyone else." Emma pauses. "I hope it all works out for you."

"Me too!" And I realize at that moment, I really do.

"Hey, we need to go shopping next week before your date. Get you a killer outfit, get your hair and nails done, the works!" Emma suggests.

"Oh, I wish I could, but I really don't have the extra funds. Since the clubhouse burned down, I've lost a lot of money from tips from the bar. Things will pick back up when we move into the new clubhouse, but until then, I need to watch what I spend."

"I'm sorry, Honey. I didn't realize." She pauses and then asks, "Will you let me treat you? It would mean the world to me if you would."

"Why? Why would you want to do that?" *Is this girl for real?* I'm totally shocked by her offer.

"Well, there are a lot of things that you may or may not know about me. First of all, my family is loaded, which practically guarantees that I'll always have money. I have two trust funds and I earn a living. I know it sounds snooty, but money has never been a problem for me. I'm not one to spend money frivolously, but if I can spend some money on a friend to cheer her up or make her day, I'll do it. So, what do you say? Will you let me treat you to a girl's day out?"

"You would really do that for me?"

"Of course I would. What is the point of having all this money if I can't spend it to make a friend happy?"

I laugh. "It's a date!"

"Woohoo!" she exclaims. I am slowly finding out what it's like to have a true girlfriend.

Emma gets a lost look on her face and I ask, "Emma, are you ok?"

"Yeah, I was just thinking that the last time I had a girl's day out was with Brianne. It just makes me sad to think of all that she has endured because of Cade and me. Mark would never have targeted her if she weren't connected to me. I feel so guilty knowing that she is addicted to drugs and lying in a hospital bed totally out of it because of me."

"Can you go visit her?"

"Cade says not yet. Apparently, she is going through a detox right now and isn't herself, so to speak," she says.

"Oh, I see. I'm all too familiar with the whole detox thing. It's rough. I'm sorry." I pause and then add, "If you wouldn't mind, I'd like to go with you when you do visit her."

"I would love that. I think I'm going to need all the moral support I can get, especially with Cade being gone. He said Hawk will be monitoring her progress while he is in Ireland and that Hawk will let me know when I can go see her."

"Honey, if you are sure you don't need any help, I'm gonna try to get some work done."

"Absolutely, hun. You do what you need to do."

She grabs her laptop and sets it up on the open spot on the counter, get herself a glass of tea, and turns from girlfriend to work mode.

CHAPTER 16

At 6:30 pm, Emma and I both hear Ice's Harley pull in the drive. He comes in the house and goes straight to Emma. "Hey, beautiful," he says as he walks over to her and kisses the top of her head lovingly. "Honey, that smells wonderful. I'm famished." He adds, "Reb and Hawk should be right behind me. They made a stop at the liquor store on the way. And the rest of the boys are coming behind them."

"Oh, good," I reply. "Dinner is just about ready."

"I didn't fuck things up by inviting the boys, did I?" he asks.

"Naw. You know me, Ice, I'm used to cooking for an army. We have plenty," I tell him. He sits down next to Emma and begins to inquire about her day. I work at putting the finishing touches on dinner so that everything will be ready when everyone gets here.

Not long after Ice returned, in walk Ari, Rebel, and Hawk. Ari had gone into to town to run some errands—she must have returned just as Hawk and Rebel arrived. Rebel has his arm around Ari lovingly ... it's good to see them both happy. Not long after their arrival, the rest of the boys filter in. The house is now full of noise and laughter. I sure have missed this. It was always like this at the clubhouse, but since the explosion...well, things have been different. It's nice to see things falling back to some type of normalcy.

"Dinner's ready," I call out from the kitchen.

"Great, just let me drop these bags in my room and I'll be right out," Ari says.

"Honey, that smells amazing," Hawk says as he strolls into the kitchen. He comes up behind me and kisses me on my neck. My body tingles at his touch.

"I'll give you a hand," Rebel says as he follows Ari into her room.

During dinner, Rebel tells us a little about his parents and family, but when the conversation gets too involved, Ice quickly stops him and changes the subject. Instead, we talk about Ari leaving for school in the morning. She is not happy about it, but Ice insists. And like a good sister, she doesn't protest.

When dinner is over, Ari and Emma help me clean up. The majority of the club leaves after thanking me for a good meal.

Hawk and Rebel remain with Ice as they take their scotch and cigars and head for the game room. They start a game of pool as they smoke and drink.

After the kitchen is spotless, we join the guys and watch Ice and Hawk finish their game. When Hawk wins, he suggests that the girls play the guys. *Oh, I'm down for that.* It's a good thing us girls are not competitive where pool is concerned. The guys, on the other hand, are. Well, at least at first—but then Emma and I kept them laughing so much, I think they forgot to care.

When we are done playing, Ice announces that he and Emma are calling it a night.

"Yeah," Hawk says, "I need to go, too." He looks over to me. "Walk me out?" he asks me. I smile as we walk toward the door.

My heart soars as I walk out of the house with Hawk. When we get to his bike he just stares at me as he continues to hold onto my hand.

"Is this really gonna happen?" he asks.

I nod and reply, "I hope so."

"And Ice?"

"I'm not gonna lie to you; I have feelings for Ice. I always have." I see his expression turn from hopeful to disappointment and it breaks my heart, but he needs to understand. "Baby, look at me." He does, and I continue. "You, more than anyone, know what a mess I was when I came to this club. Ice is my savior because he gave me a home and a family. I thought I was in love with him. But when Emma came back, I realized that although it may be love, it's not the kind of love that he has for Emma or that I have always had for you. He may have been my savior, but you were always my confidant, my rock, and as I'm slowly learning, my love." I'm not being completely honest with Hawk, but I want him to understand that Ice is my past and he is my future. Hopefully, we can build on that.

"I needed to hear that," he says.

"And I needed to say it."

He caresses the side of my cheek and then says, "When you hooked up with Ice, I thought we were done. He is my prez and best friend, and there was no way I was going to interfere with that. I couldn't go against my prez. But then Emma came into the picture and I realized that he had been in love with her all his life. She was the woman for him. As much as I hated seeing you hurting, I was hopeful. But you had already pushed me so far out of your life I didn't know what to think."

"I'm sorry, I should never have pushed you away. But I never wanted there to be any trouble between you and Ice. So I felt that keeping my distance would make things easier."

He wraps his arm around my waist and pulls me close against him. "Are you still pushing me away?" he asks breathlessly.

"No," I reply, feeling his hot breath against my lips as he bends down to kiss me. At first, his lips are soft, hesitant, as if he is afraid that I will push him away. But when a moan escapes my lips, he knows there is no way in hell I'm pushing him away and he deepens the kiss, pulling me closer and ravaging my mouth.

Instinctively, I wrap my arms around his neck and my body molds against him. I can feel his erection pushing against my core as my tongue meets every desperate stroke of his tongue. I want him to take me right here, so I reach for the buckle of his belt. His hand immediately goes to my hand to stop me.

"Oh God, Honey," he pleads. "I want this, God knows how much I want this, but I'm saying no. Not in Ice's driveway."

"But ..." I interrupt, but he quickly stops me from saying any more.

"Our first time is gonna be special, as it should be. It's definitely not happening in Ice's home, his porch, his yard, or his fucking driveway."

I giggle at his words as I realize he's right. I don't want our first time to be here.

"You're laughing at me," he says, surprised.

Smiling, I reply, "No babe, not laughing at you. Laughing 'cause you are right. Thank you."

He smiles back. "I gotta go, babe. See you tomorrow."

"You got it, big guy," I reply. He kisses me on the cheek and proceeds to mount his bike. Revving the engine and placing his helmet on his head, he waves and drives off.

God, I love that man, I think to myself as I walk back into the house. And I realize that I am hopeful for our future together. And then a scary thought enters my mind: am I in love with him, or do I just love the idea of him? I shake my head. *No! This is gonna work.*

"Good morning, ladies," Ice says as he comes into the kitchen the next morning.

"Good morning, babe," Emma says as she walks over to him and gives him a kiss.

"Ari, are ya ready to go?" he asks.

"I am. Rebel was over this morning and helped me pack the car. It was tough saying goodbye, but he said that as soon as he gets back from Ireland he would come down and see me."

"Oh, I bet he will," he says sarcastically. "Promise me you'll be careful? You know I worry."

"Yes, Caden, I promise. You tell me all the time that I drive like a grandma. I don't think I can get any more careful than that," she says smartly. He laughs. Then she adds, "I was just waiting for you to get your butt out of bed so I could say goodbye before I left." She walks over to him and gives him a big hug.

"I'll call you when I get back to the States."

"Promise you'll be safe."

"I promise."

"Promise me something else?" she asks.

"Anything."

"Keep Rebel safe. Please bring him home to me, Caden." She sounds so scared and desperate. I feel bad for her and Emma. They are so worried about Ice and Rebel and I totally can understand that. I'm worried for them too, but we all have seen them survive the impossible and I have to keep the faith that they will survive this as well and come home to the women that love them.

Ari gives Emma and me a hug and turns to leave with tears in her eyes. I know that she wants to stay and I whisper to her, "Just one more semester, sweetie. You got this." She nods and walks out the door.

After Ari leaves, Emma excuses herself and runs upstairs, which leaves Ice and me alone. I'm sure it's another bout of morning sickness.

We are silent for several minutes and then Ice asks, "Will you do me a favor, Honey?"

"Sure, Ice. I would do anything for you."

"I want you to take care of Emma for me while I am gone. I have no idea how long we'll be gone, and it'll really make me feel better knowing that she has you as well as the club looking after her."

"Ice, there's no need for you to even ask that. Emma and I have built a true friendship and I've already planned on staying around here with her while you're away. You don't need to worry about her at all."

"Thank you. I knew I could count on you," he replies, relieved.

"Count on her for what?" Emma says as she comes back into the kitchen.

"Not a thing," he says.

"If you're talking about having Honey babysit me, I think she's beat you to the punch and has already planned on doing that."

He laughs. "So you were eavesdropping?"

"No, I wasn't, but I know you, Caden Jackson. For some reason, you seem to think that I can't take care of myself. So even though I can, I will indulge your insecurities and allow Honey to babysit me."

"Fuck, I'm gonna miss you, girl!" he says as he pulls her in for a kiss.

I go about making myself busy in the kitchen as they say their goodbyes. When he's ready to leave he comes over to me and gives me a slight hug and says, "Take care, girl—and remember your promise."

"You got it, boss. Be safe!" I reply as the fucking tears fight to break free. But I hold them in like I always do.

Emma immerses herself in her work and I clean. I don't think Ice had been gone fifteen minutes before we felt the loss. I'm sure we will be seeing other members of the club from time to time, but that doesn't make it easier. Emma is asleep on the couch, so I decide to clean the upstairs so I don't disturb her. She needs her sleep.

Just as I finish the upstairs, I faintly hear my name being called. I come downstairs and see Emma standing at the bottom of the steps. "What are you doing?" she asks.

"Cleaning,"

"Why?"

"Well, unlike you, I don't have work to dig into. So I do what I do best: cook and clean." I come all the way down the steps and walk over to the cupboard to put the duster away. I turn back toward Emma and say, "Now, what were you saying about running to the store?"

"Oh, yeah. I'm going stir-crazy waiting to hear if the boys landed; I need to get out of this house. Wanna come?"

"Sure, let me just run a brush through my hair and I'll meet you outside."

"Ok." Emma grabs her purse and heads for the door.

When I get outside, Emma is standing by her car with a note in her hand. She's trembling and I immediately know that something is wrong. But I don't say anything and just proceed with caution, following her lead.

"Come on girl, shopping awaits. Get in the car," she says. I can tell that she is putting on an act. Are we being watched?

After closing the door, I ask, "What the fuck is going on, Emma? Your whole demeanor just changed. You're scaring me."

"Just act normal until we get away from the house. Then I will tell you everything."

After we get away from the driveway and out onto the main road, she hands me a note.

I know what you did.

I know what he did.

You will not get away with it.

And neither will he.

What in the hell is going on? Who could have sent this? "Holy fuck, Emma! Where did you get this?"

"It was on my windshield." She looks over at me and I can see that she is terrified. "Call Hawk. Please," she begs.

I immediately pull out my phone and begin dialing. When it starts to ring, I put it on speaker phone.

One, two three rings. *Why isn't he answering?* Four, five six rings ... and it goes to his voicemail. *Fuck!*

"What do I do?" she asks me.

"Let's drive by Betty's and see if he's there. Maybe he's in a meeting or something and can't get to the phone."

"Ok," I reply. She changes direction and heads toward Waterford.

A few minutes later, my phone rings. I look down and say, "It's Hawk." I answer the phone and put him on speaker.

"What's up, babe? Sorry I missed your call. I was on the line with Ice. They just landed in Dublin," he says into the phone.

"That's great, Hawk. Glad to hear they're safe. Emma too. Speaking of Emma, she needs to talk to you. I have you on speaker, we're in her car."

"Hey doll, what's up?" Hawk says to Emma.

"Hawk, someone left a note on my car. It's not good. Honey and I decided to run to the store and when I walked out to the car I saw a piece of paper on my windshield. Thinking nothing of it, I grabbed it and began to read it. Hawk, someone was watching me while I read that note! What do I do?"

He asks no questions, just calmly says, "I'm at Betty's. You and Honey get here as quick as you can—and make sure you bring the note!"

"We're already on the way. I have the note. Thanks, Hawk," she says and I can hear the relief in her voice.

I hang up and we continue to drive straight to Betty's. We arrive fifteen minutes later.

I lead Emma into the diner and head straight for the back and up the stairs. I know exactly where Hawk is keeping himself and so I go directly to his makeshift office.

"Let me see it," he says as we walk into the room. She hands him the note and he begins to read. When he's done, he asks, "Do you recognize the handwriting?"

Instead of answering him, she blurts out, "Hawk, I know what this is about."

He looks at her curiously. "You do?"

"Yes. This has to do with Grayson," she says confidently.

"What makes you say that?"

"Well, the handwriting reminds me of Mark. Now, I know that it is not his handwriting, but once I thought of him I made the connection. What else have both Cade and I done recently? We just reconnected after eleven years. This has to be about Grayson. There isn't anything else it could be."

"You might have a point there. To an extent, it makes sense. But I need to look into this further to be sure," he says.

"Tell me, is there anyone that you know—maybe a member of the Satans club—who was friends with Mark? Maybe that Skid guy?" Emma asks.

"Yeah, I think they were friends," Hawk says.

"And does Skid know that Caden killed Mark? Does he know that I was kidnapped and that Caden did it for me?"

"He does," he replies slowly. I finally get where she is going with this and I think Hawk is too.

He says, "Alright, I'll check it out." He pauses and adds, "In the meantime, when you talk to Ice—who, by the way, said he would be calling you tonight—don't say anything to him about this right now. I'll put some guys on the house and make sure that you all are watched."

"Why can't I say anything to Caden?" she asks.

"Emma, he is dealing with some nasty shit in Ireland. I know he didn't tell you everything, but I don't want him worrying about anything but getting the fuck home. If he knew about the note, he will feel torn and will want to rush home to you—and I get that, really I do. But until we know more, I don't want to alarm him. This could be nothing."

"Ok, I understand."

Hawk pulls out his phone and dials. He says, "Hey, I need you and Dbag to plan on spending a lot of time with Emma. She does not leave Ice's lake house or go anywhere without the both of you with her. You will be staying there, too, so plan on moving in for a while."

He waits while the person on the line responds and then says, "She's with me at Betty's right now. I'll keep her here until you get here." He pauses. "And Spike, you both protect her with your life. You got me?"

After Hawk is done on the phone he walks over to Emma and gives her a hug, kissing the top of my head. "Everything is going to be ok, darl'n. I promise. I won't let anything happen to you, not on my watch. Besides, Ice would have my head." He chuckles and then adds, "I'll make contact with the Satans and see what I can find out about Skid, too. You need to go back to the house, though. I don't want you roaming around town until I know something more concrete about this." He looks over to me as if to ask me to also keep an eye on her. I nod and show him that I am with him on this.

"Ok, Hawk. Thank you."

"Dbag and Spike will be coming by to escort you ladies home." He walks over to me and pulls me into a hug. "Even though the circumstances suck, I can't tell you how nice it is to see you, babe." He kisses me on the cheek and I can't help but giggle. I have to say that I am thoroughly enjoying his attention. *Why didn't I agree to this earlier?* I ask myself and then I quickly remember why: Ice.

Emma and I make our way downstairs and a few minutes later, Hawk joins us. Emma turns to him and asks, "So Cade called?"

"Yes. They just landed in Dublin," he says as he looks at his watch, "about an hour ago. They're heading over to get transport to Belfast."

"Transport?" she asks.

"Yeah, one of the Knights sister clubs in Belfast arranged for them to have bikes. You know how Ice hates driving in a cage."

We laugh and it helps relieve some of the tension from earlier. I can tell that Emma is still concerned by all this and she confirms my suspicions when she asks, "Hawk, do you think we should be worried about this note?"

"Emma, I really don't know. Give me some time to look into it further. The precautions I'm taking are preemptive and reactive. I don't want to think nothing of it and have it turn out to be something. This way, I have you protected from the get-go."

"Ok, I trust you."

About an hour later, Spike shows up at Betty's. He walks over to our table and says, "Reporting for babysitting duty, boss."

Smartass.

Hawk stands up and gets into Spike's face. "You get this straight, brother: Emma is our prez's old lady. You will protect her as you would protect him or any brother in this club, and you will not disrespect her. Understood?"

Holy shit, is he really mad?

Spike says, "Hawk, man, I was just messing with her. I know who she is and I know how much she means to our prez. You don't have to remind me."

"Then remember this isn't a joke or a game at Emma's expense," Hawk says.

"I got it, geez." He looks over at me and then says, "I'm sorry, Emma. I meant no disrespect."

"See, that wasn't so hard," Hawk says sarcastically.

"Fuck you. She knew I was messing with her. You just made a big deal out of nothing," Spike says.

"Do we need to go a few rounds outside?" Hawk asks.

Nope, he's teasing.

"Sure, old man! Let's do it. I'll kick your ass," Spike replies.

"Guys, guys, stop this!" Emma yells. I think she actually thinks they are about to throw down right here in Betty's. I can't hold it in any longer and I bust out laughing.

"What?" Emma asks.

Now we're all laughing. "Why are you all laughing?" she asks. She seems genuinely hurt that we are laughing.

I can't let her suffer any longer and I speak up and explain. "Emma, we're laughing 'cause they were just messing with each other and you thought they were going to start fighting. They do this all the time. I'm sorry for laughing; you didn't know."

"Oh," she looks over to me. "Will I ever get this?" she asks and damn it, I feel bad for her.

"Of course you will, you're doing better than most in your situation would. This is all new to you—we get that. But we'll get you there, I promise. You're good for Ice and we aren't going to let you fail."

"Hell no!" Hawk replies. He looks at me and smiles. I think he is pleased that I am so willing to help Emma get all this. I think it gives him a bit of the security that he needed to get past my relationship with Ice.

CHAPTER 17

On the way back to the house, I notice that Emma seems to have relaxed a bit about the whole note thing. Dbag and Spike follow us back on their bikes. When we get to the house, she parks the car and we get out. She pauses and looks around warily, then shudders and goes inside. *Ok, so she's on edge again.*

We all walk into the house and once the door is closed and locked, she turns to Spike and says, "Spike, I know this might sound a bit paranoid, but I think it is important for you to know that when I discovered the note on my car I was sure that someone was in the trees watching and listening."

"You sure? You don't think that maybe you were just freaked out by the note?" he asks.

"At first, I did think that, but then a feeling came over me. You know, that one where your stomach falls to the grounds and your skin begins to prickle? I would bet money that someone was there."

"Ok, darl'n. Dbag and I will go check it out."

"Thank you."

They pull out their guns and hold them at their sides as they walk out the door. I have to say, I'm getting the heebie-jeebies too. I am quite glad they are both here.

A few minutes later the guys return. Spike says, "Well, Miss Emma, I don't want to scare you more than you already are, but I think you're right. There is a pile of cigarette butts behind the tree over by the driveway. If any of our guys were out here, they wouldn't be hiding in the trees and wouldn't need to hide their cigarette butts." He starts walking through the house and making sure that all the windows and doors in the house are locked. "You ladies don't go outside for anything. Not even the mail. You hear me?" We both nod.

Just then Emma's phone starts to ring. She walks over to her bag and pulls it out. She smiles and answers, "Hey, handsome!"

I turn to Spike and say, "That better be Ice, for all our sakes," and we all laugh.

Emma comes back into the kitchen and Spike asks, "Was that Ice?"

"Yes. They made it to Belfast."

He mimes clearing his brow in relief and says, "Good." Dbag and I smirk as he walks over to Emma and puts his arm around her, giving her a slight squeeze. "He'll be home before you and that baby know it."

Spike is a good guy. He always knows the right thing to say. Unfortunately, I can't take stock in his reassurance. I'm worried for Ice and the boys. I try my best to keep my feelings about them hidden from Emma. The last thing she needs right now is to worry more than she already does.

"Thanks, sweetie. Hopefully, you're right." She pauses and then says, "This whole note thing has got me worried. Hawk says not to bother Caden with it, but all my instincts are shouting at me to tell him."

"Trust Hawk. He has been around the block a few times and knows what he's doing. His first priority is his loyalty to Ice. He won't steer you wrong."

"Yeah, when you put it like that it does make it a little easier to accept."

"So, Honey girl, whatcha cooking me and Dbag for dinner?" Spike asks.

I laugh. "Who says I am cooking you boys anything?"

"Awww, come on, Honey. We've missed your cooking since the clubhouse blew." He then adds, "Besides, we're your protection. You gotta keep us nourished, right?"

I love taking care of these boys. They have always made me feel welcome and needed around here and I would do anything to keep them happy. So of course, I cave. I was actually planning on making them dinner anyway, but I just wanted to tease him a little. "I think I am going to make some chili. Does that sound good?"

"Oh, hell yeah!" Spike cheers.

"Fucking A! That sounds awesome, Honey. Can we help?" Dbag adds.

I chuckle to myself. There's nothing like a home-cooked meal to turn these big bad bikers into happy boys. They're not so tough after all.

"Naw, Emma and I got this. You boys go hang out in there or shoot some pool or just do whatever it is you boys do." I shoo them off.

We finish dinner and Emma and I clean up the kitchen. When all is said and done, the boys check the house and grounds, then double-check that all the doors and windows are locked. When the house is secure, we all turn in for the night. Spike takes the room that Rebel slept in while he was here last week and Dbag sleeps on the couch.

Emma offered him one of the other guest rooms, but he was insistent that it would be better if he were out in the living space in case he was needed.

The house is quiet and then we hear Emma scream.

We all run up to the third floor and Spike yells, "What the hell, Emma? What's happened?"

"Whoever left the note this morning has been in the house. Look." She points to a rose and a note on the bed. It appears that it hasn't been opened. Spike walks over to the note while putting his riding gloves on. With his gloved hand, he picks up the note and begins to read.

Your biker friends can't protect you.

Your biker boyfriend will go down with you.

When he finishes reading the note he pulls out his cell phone and dials. He holds the phone to his ear and a few seconds later begins to speak. "Hawk, hey. We've got a problem. Emma got another note."

He's listening to Hawk on the other end and then reads the note to Hawk. He listens some more and then says, "Ok, see you soon." He disconnects the line and looks over at Emma. "He's on his way."

Emma pushes past us and runs down the stairs. We hear the glass shattering before we see it and when we get downstairs, we see that she has thrown a beer bottle. She's frantically running around the house breaking glasses and bottles in her wake. Spike grabs her arm to stop her.

"Whoa there, darl'n. I think you have made your point."

"Let me throw it. It makes me feel better!" she yells.

"I know. I know it does. But you're making a mess and frankly, I don't think you or anyone else wants to clean it up," Spike says. He then adds, "I'm glad you're angry and I am glad that you're reacting to this as you are. But let's refocus that energy into finding this asshole and ending him once and for all." He takes a beer bottle out of her hand and takes it over to the kitchen counter.

He walks back over to her and says, "Are you feeling better now?" I am shocked by her behavior. She's always so passive; I have never seen her truly angry.

"I'm not a victim!" she states. She places her hands on her belly as if to reassure her child that everything is going to be alright.

I walk over to her and give her a hug. "Emma, we know that you're not a victim. Hawk will get this guy, I just know it."

"She's right, Emma. We'll get him," Dbag adds.

A few minutes later there's a knock at the door. Spike goes over to the door, looks out the side window, and then opens the door. Hawk hurriedly walks in and comes straight over to Emma. "Are you ok?"

"I'm fine," she says. "Thanks for coming over this late."

"It's not a problem at all. Ice left your care in my hands and I won't let my brother down. So, what can you tell me about this last note?"

"Not much, really. I had gone up to bed and as soon as I walked into the bedroom and flicked on the light I saw the rose laying on my pillow and the piece of paper next to it. I didn't even touch it; I just reacted with a scream."

"A blood-curdling scream," I add. It's probably not the most opportune moment to comment, but she scared the living shit out of me.

She looks over at me. "Sorry, I didn't mean to scare you." She turns back to Hawk and says, "When I screamed, everyone showed up in my room. Spike went over and picked up the note and read it. I don't have anything else."

"Spike, first thing in the morning, you get these fucking locks changed." He turns back to Emma and says, "Emma, what can you tell me about Mark Grayson that I don't already know?"

"Hell, I don't know, Hawk. I really thought I knew the man, but over the course of the last several weeks I realize that I never really knew him at all."

"Does he have any other family that you can think of?"

"He had an aunt in New York that he spoke of once or twice, but not regularly and not enough for me to ask about her."

"Friends?"

"Nope, no friends. Well, except Skid, but we didn't know that until a couple of weeks ago. Do you think Skid could be doing this?"

"Possibly, but I doubt it."

"Why not Skid?"

"Well, it's not a biker move. We don't play games. If we're trying to get a point across or threaten someone, we just do it. Skid may be an asshole, but he's all biker. This isn't his style. His ego is too big to hide in the shadows."

"Should we call the police?"

Spike looks at Hawk and says, "You know, it wouldn't hurt to let Briggs know what's going on here. Hell, he might even be able to help."

No, no, no! I've managed to avoid him this long. Not now, where I have nowhere to hide! Trying to sway Hawk against that idea, I say, "Why would you even think about getting the police involved, Hawk? That's not you ... and that's definitely not something Ice would do."

"I agree," Hawk says and I'm relieved for a moment. Then he throws me for a loop when he adds, "With Spike." He's quiet for a moment and then says, "Emma, I want you to think real hard. Is there something that we're missing? Did someone come into the house since the last time you were upstairs?"

I can't take any more. I definitely cannot face Jack. I run from the room and make a beeline to my room. *Maybe they won't notice that I left and I can just stay here until he leaves. This can't be happening. It just can't. I'm not ready!*

A few minutes later, I hear a knock at my bedroom door. "Honey? Are you ok?" Emma asks.

I have no choice but to open the door. I'm gonna have to face this sooner or later. Emma walks in and says, "Honey?"

"I'm right here," I say in the darkness.

"Are you ok? You seemed a little upset when Hawk mentioned calling Briggs."

"Emma, you have enough to worry about right now. You don't need to add my problems to the mix."

"Honey, you're my friend. Hawk has my situation under control. What's going on with you?"

"Oh, Emma, I don't know what to do." I sit down on the bed and sigh.

"Why don't you tell me and maybe I can help?"

"Remember when Hawk said that he was calling Sgt. Briggs?"

"Yes."

"I have a sketchy past with Sgt. Briggs."

"Sketchy? What could you have possibly done that's worse than the rest of us?"

I look at her sadly and say, "Trust me, it's worse."

"It can't be all that bad. Why don't you give me a shot? I won't say anything to the guys if you don't want me to."

"I know you won't, and it would really help to talk about it, but I don't want you to treat me differently because of it."

"Really?" she says. "These boys kill people, run illegal guns, and Lord knows what else. Are you a gunrunner?" I shake my head. "You didn't kill someone, did you?" I can't help the smile that comes across my face as I shake my head.

"Edinboro is my hometown. But when I was in my twenties, I left. I had a bad coke problem; really bad. I did some of the most unimaginable things to myself and other people. Things I don't want to relive or even talk about."

"Ok, go on," she urges.

"Briggs and I went to school together. We started out as really good friends, then we dated, and eventually, we were engaged. Up until that time, I'd done really well at hiding my drug problem. I would only shoot up when I was alone, after ensuring that I wouldn't be seeing anyone for a while. But after we got engaged and all the pressure started to build, the drugs began to take over my life. I lied to so many people. I stole money from my family, my friends, and even Briggs. I played so many cons just to get my next fix. And if the opportunity would have ever presented itself, I'm sure I would have killed for drug money too. I killed my unborn child because I was so strung out on drugs, I couldn't handle having a having a baby in my state of despair."

"Honey, everyone has some problem or another that they're dealing with. Some are just worse than others. You had an addiction; something you were unable to control. I'm sorry about the abortion, but you were not in your right mind. Why would you beat yourself up about this?"

I don't answer her direct question but continue with my story, "The night before my wedding, I needed a fix so bad. I'd spent every last dime I had, borrowed from everyone I knew, and stole all the money I could get my hands on. On this particular night, pre-wedding jitters were getting the best of me and I had nothing. I was sitting on my bed and I looked down at my shaking hands. And there was my answer. My beautiful two-caret diamond engagement ring glistened on my left hand."

I look over at her, waiting to hear the words that I dread, but instead, she pulls me into a hug and says, "What happened next?"

"I went straight to a pawn shop and pawned my ring off for a measly $100 fix. I never showed up for my wedding. I just left Jack standing at the altar, waiting for me to walk down the aisle. When I sobered up enough to realize what I had done, I couldn't face anyone. So I packed my shit and left town. A month later, I killed our child. I have not seen or spoken to him since."

"Honey, you were young and you had an addiction. You've taken the first steps by admitting that you had a problem; you can't beat yourself up about them. I'm sure Sgt. Briggs will understand, but you need to talk to him. You need to explain to him."

"I doubt he would ever talk to me again."

"Does he know you've come back to town?"

"I doubt it. I have not kept in touch with any of my friends from that time. That's why I am always at the clubhouse. The MC has become a haven for me. When I told you that Ice took me in and saved my life, it wasn't an exaggeration. It's the truth."

"Do you still have feelings for Sgt. Briggs?"

"I really don't know. I'm not sure if my feelings for Briggs are true, or if they come from shame and guilt. Right now, it's Hawk that I want. And when he finds out he's not going to want to have anything to do with me," I say, and the tears that I have been holding back for so long begin to fall.

"That's not true. He'll understand and so will Sgt. Briggs. You just need to talk to them both." Just then there is a knock at the door. Emma opens the door and Hawk is standing at the doorway, staring at me. The look on his face is one of total confusion. "I think I need to talk to Spike about something," Emma says as she turns toward the door. "You two need to talk." She looks over to me and mouths, "Talk to him!" And then she leaves the room.

Hawk stares at me intently while Emma slowly closes the door behind her.

"So, do you want to fill me in on what's going on with you?" he asks as he sits down on the bed next to me.

I know he needs to be told about my past and I have every intention of doing so, I just don't want to have this conversation now. But really, at this point, what choice do I have?

"Do you remember when I first came to the club?" I ask.

"Yeah, of course, I do. You were a mess. You had just gotten out of rehab and were still coping with your addiction."

"I was. You and the rest of the club knew about my addiction and the steps I had taken to overcome it. This club supported me and stood by me during some of my worst days."

"Yeah, we did. You're telling me stuff that I already know, babe. What you aren't telling me is why you are crying now."

I grab a tissue off the nightstand and wipe my eyes and blow my nose. It's not one of my more attractive moments, but this is Hawk. He's the man who has seen me at my worst and still wants to be with me. I pray that when I tell him the rest of this story he will still feel that way.

"Yes, I know. But you don't know everything from my past. There are things that I purposely left out because I didn't want your opinion of me to change. But you, more than anyone else, need to know these things. And since my past is about to come back and bite me in the ass, I need to tell you before that happens."

I proceed to tell him everything that I told Emma about Jack, my addiction, stealing, my ring, and not showing up for my own wedding and the abortion. I explain to him that I disappeared that night and never turned back until I ended up on the road outside of the clubhouse the day Ice found me.

When I finish talking, I wait for Hawk to say something. He's silent for what seems like an eternity, but it's probably only a couple of seconds. "Holy shit, babe, what in the hell made you think that I would think differently about you?"

"Um, I don't know, maybe because I did some pretty shitty things to my friends, my family, and my fiancé. Not to mention the fact that I was engaged to another man and almost married him—a man that has been a long-standing friend of this club. I don't know, maybe I'm overreacting, but that seems like a lot of shit to overlook."

He puts his arm around me and pulls me in close. "Honey, sweetheart, we all know how drugs can take over a person. Many of the things you did were because of the drugs. The important thing for all of us to remember is that you did the right thing by taking responsibility and getting help. You put your life back together. Nobody expects anything more from you, especially me."

"Really?"

"Babe, of course. What kind of guy would I be if I didn't understand what you went through? What kind of guy would I be if I blamed you for those actions?"

"Thank you!" I say as the tears start to fall again.

"Everything is going to be alright." He's quiet for a minute and then adds, "But I do have to know one thing."

"Sure, anything."

"Do you still have feelings for Briggs?"

I smile. "No, I don't. I think leaving him at the altar was a blessing in disguise."

He nods. "That's good. I really didn't want to have to shoot our number one ally on the force."

I chuckle, hug him, and give him a big kiss on the cheek. "You know, you really are something special."

"Of course I know that. It's about damn time you realized it. Now let's go back out and get this threat shit settled."

"Yes, sir!"

When we come back to the living room, Emma catches me and mouths, "Everything good?" I smile and nod.

CHAPTER 18

When Sgt. Briggs arrives at the house, he immediately begins asking a lot of questions about what happened. He asks Emma if she knows what the note is referring to when it states, "I know what you did," but she plays dumb and says no. *Good girl. She is definitely learning.*

It doesn't take Briggs long to spot me and I can't help but notice the surprise on his face. I have to say, I expected his reaction. But he continues to question Emma without missing a beat. He then turns to me and says, "Amanda, anything you want to add?"

Hearing him say my name causes a shiver, but it quickly passes. If he only knew the guilt that I harbor for what I did to him. I notice that he has a wedding band on, which makes me happy. I always hoped that he would find another and it looks like he did. One of these days, maybe he and I can talk over coffee.

Hawk makes it a point to show Briggs exactly who I belong to. He's being extra affectionate. The caveman in him emerges and he's being perfectly clear by his actions that he has definitely staked his claim on me. I'm not sure what to think about his claim. Part of me likes it—hell, who wouldn't like to belong to a man like Hawk? The other part of me feels smothered and wants to say something to counter his actions. But I don't.

Sgt. Briggs leaves with a full incident report and says that he'll get his men on it right away. I think he suspects we know more than we told him, but nobody in that room was going to call their prez out for murder.

The next day, I call Jack Briggs and ask him to meet me for lunch. It's time that we talk and if I don't do it now, I never will. He agrees to meet me outside of town at a small mom and pop diner called Joe's.

I get there before him and wait. My nerves are shot and I decide to leave, but he comes walking in just as I'm about to stand up. He approaches the booth that I'm sitting in and says, "Hello, Amanda."

"Hi, Jack. Why don't you have a seat?"

He sits down and says, "Imagine my surprise when I walk into Caden's house and find you there. You were the last person I expected to see."

"I know, Jack. I'm sorry."

"How long have you been back in town?"

"A few years."

"Holy shit, Amanda! And this is the first time we're talking?"

"I'm a coward, Jack. I've always been a coward, but it's time I come clean about everything. There are so many things that you don't know, but they're things you need to know."

"I'm listening."

Just then the waitress comes by to take our order and we both order coffee. I look up, hoping that perhaps he's changed his mind and doesn't want to listen, but he looks at me eagerly, encouraging me to tell him everything.

I take a deep breath and begin, "I am a recovering drug addict." He gasps. I was so good at hiding the truth from him, I don't think he even suspected. "The night I left town, I pawned my engagement ring for a quick fix." He's silent, so I add, "I know now that there is no excuse for what I did, but back then, I didn't care. All I wanted was to get high. That was all I could think about. I was nervous about the wedding and my future. I had spent so much time keeping the drugs from you and I was literally freaking out about how I was going to continue to do that after we were married."

"I never knew," he says sadly.

"Please understand, it wasn't that I didn't love you. I did. But unfortunately, I loved myself more. I only cared about what I wanted. I didn't care who I hurt in the process, including you."

"You broke me, Amanda. It took me a long time to get over you and your disappearance. I tried to find you, but couldn't. I even think that I joined the force so that I had access to their resources. Everything was a dead end."

"I went to New York. I covered my tracks. My drug dealer set me up with a fake ID and I lived under a different name for years."

He looks down at the table. "Are you better now?"

"Yes. After doing some time in rehab, I came back to town. I ran into Ice my first day back and he offered me a job and a place to live. It was the easy answer and so I jumped on it."

"So the MC is good to you?"

"Yes, they are."

"I got married last year." He looks down at his wedding band. "She's a wonderful woman and I love her deeply. So I guess everything worked out."

"No, Jack, it didn't."

He gives me a curious glance. "What do you mean?"

Now comes the hardest part. But I've got him here and I told myself I would tell him everything. If I am ever going to move on, I have to follow through. I take another deep breath and say, "There is one last thing that you need to know."

"What's done is done. There is no reason to rehash what might have been or what you did or what I did. We've both moved on."

"No, Jack, you don't understand." I look down at my hands as the tears begin to fall.

When he realizes that I am crying, he reaches for my hands, which are folded and intertwined with each other on the table. "Amanda, what is it?"

The concern in his voice breaks my heart; it tells me he still cares about me. I will never understand why. But I also know that he will never forgive me if I go on. *If I don't say anything, he will never find out. He really doesn't need to know, does he?* And then the hard voice of reason speaks to me and tells me what I already know. *You have to do this if you ever want to move on and live your life. You will never be happy if you don't.* And the voice is absolutely right.

"Jack, about a month after I got to New York, I found out that I was pregnant."

He shakes his head. "Why are you telling me this, Amanda? You had left me. Do you really think that I expected you to be faithful to me?"

"You don't understand. I hadn't been with anyone after you for a very long time." I grin ruefully and say, "Actually, it was about a year ago, but that's not the point I'm trying to make."

When the realization hits him, his eyes shine with eager brightness. His smile is heartbreaking. Beaming, he says, "Are you telling me that I have a son ... or a daughter? Amanda, do we?"

I can't stop crying. My heart broke when I killed my child and now it is breaking all over again as I'm about to tell its father that I killed him or her. How do I tell him that I have no idea if it was a boy or a girl? How do I tell him that I don't know who it looked like, or if it was a good baby or fussy? I will never know because I didn't have the courage to fight for my child.

Finally I say, "No, Jack, we don't."

He looks confused. "I don't understand."

"Jack, my state of mind at the time, it was off the charts. I ..."

He doesn't let me finish and interrupts, "Oh God, Amanda ... tell me you didn't."

I'm so ashamed. I can't look at him. I can't even respond. My silence is confirmation of his worst fear, and he says, "God damn you, Amanda. How could you?"

I still can't respond. I have no words, because nothing can tell him why I did what I did and nothing can describe to him how I feel. No words can even begin to touch the surface of my heartbreak.

"I can't even look at you," he says and then he gets up from the booth. He throws some money down on the table and then turns and walks toward the door. When he gets to the door he glances back at me and shakes his head in disgust. Turning back, he opens the door and leaves.

It's done. I really thought it would make me feel better once I told him, but I don't feel any better. Actually, I feel much worse. *Will this ache ever go away?* Every time I think about the abortion the memories make my heart ache. I relive that pain over and over again. *Will it ever stop?*

CHAPTER 19

It's been several days since Briggs and I had lunch. I have not heard from him regarding our conversation and to my knowledge, nobody has heard from him about the mystery stalker. Emma is starting to relax and I am glad to see it. I know it is early in her pregnancy, but she doesn't need to be getting herself worked up.

Today, Emma and I are having our girls' day out. I'm so excited; we're going shopping, going to the spa, etc. What more could a girl ask for? Then after that, tonight will be my first real date with Hawk.

I'm sitting at the kitchen table having coffee with Spike and Dbag when Emma comes down. She plops her purse down on the table, looks at me, and says, "Are you ready for our big day?"

Before I can answer, Spike asks, "What big day?"

She replies nonchalantly, "Honey and I are having a girl's day out today—hair, nails, makeup. The works."

"Oh, hell no!" Spike replies.

"What do you mean?"

"You ladies are NOT going out shopping and doing girly shit today. Hawk told you both to stay put!"

"We weren't planning on going alone."

"I'm not having a spa day with you girls. That would be emotional suicide for a guy like me!"

"It won't be that bad. What do you think, Dbag?" she asks teasingly.

"It sounds like fun," he says.

Spike looks over at him and says, "You're such a fucking pussy! We're not going! And that's final!"

Emma looks at me and I know exactly what she wants. I get up from my chair and together we walk over to Spike and flank him. As we place our arms around him, she asks, "But Spike, you wouldn't disappoint us, would you?" Then she adds, "Honey has a hot date with your VP tonight. You want her to look especially pretty for him, don't you?"

"It's not working, Emma. Your attempts to unman me are not gonna get me to change my mind. I said no and I mean no!" he replies.

And then Emma totally takes me by surprise and plays the old lady card. "Maybe I should remind you, Spike, that I'm Ice's old lady. You know, your club prez? I think he would be very disappointed in you if he knew you weren't willing to take his woman and her friend to the spa and shopping."

"He would agree with me if he knew about the threats," he says defensively. He's absolutely right. I have to chuckle to myself.

"But he doesn't know, does he? And Hawk won't let me tell him, so sweetie, it appears to me that if you don't take us where we want to go today, you're screwed."

Spike shakes his head in defeat. I can see that he knows he has no way out of this. "People are so wrong about bikers. They fear them when they should fear their fucking old ladies. They're the dangerous ones," Spike says.

Emma and I have a blast on our girl's day out. We start at the spa with facials, mani-pedis, and massages. Once we are all prettied up, we hit the stores, have lunch, and then return home. The boys are great sports about it all and there are even times that I think they're actually enjoying themselves, although they would never admit it.

Spike pulls into the driveway and turns the car off. We all get out of the car and walk toward the trunk. Spike opens it up and begins handing packages to Dbag as Emma and I turn the corner to head to the front door. As we approach the front porch, Emma stops dead in her tracks. When I look up at the porch, I see a basket and the fucking lid is moving.

"What the fuck is that, Emma?"

"I don't know, but I saw the lid move. There is something inside that basket, and I'm not going to be the one to find out what it is." We both back away from the steps slowly and I call as calmly as I can, "Spike?"

As he and Dbag come around the corner with all our packages, he says, "What's up, doll?"

Emma points to the steps and says, "That. There's another note. And there is something alive in that basket."

Spike walks up to the basket slowly. Just as he's about to remove the lid of the basket, we all hear the rattle. *Holy fucking shit, there's a snake in that basket.* Emma begins to hyperventilate and I go over to her to help her breathe.

Spike and Dbag both draw their guns and fire on the basket. The hail of gunfire destroys the basket and reveals the snake, still twitching, lying dead within the remnants of the basket. We wait for the muscle reflex to stop.

"A fucking rattlesnake!" Spike yells. "This asshole isn't just trying to scare you, he's trying to fucking kill you!" He walks over and grabs the note. Opening the note, he reads out loud:

Enjoy your shopping and the spa today?

I hope so because before long you will soon realize that you can run.

But you can't hide.

When your biker boyfriend returns from Ireland

Your day will come.

Holy fuck, this guy is not playing around.

Once we are inside the house and the snake is disposed of, Emma goes straight upstairs to her room.

"What's up with her?" Spike asks.

"I don't know, but I am gonna make damn sure to find out," I reply and I march up the stairs after her. I get to the doorway of her room as she is pulling a bag out of the closet. I stand there unnoticed as she begins to grab clothes from the dresser drawers and quickly stuffs them in the bag.

"Whatcha doing?" I ask.

"What's it look like?"

"You're leaving?"

"Yes."

"And where, may I ask, are you going?"

"Away."

"Not good enough. Where are you going?"

"Ireland!"

"Emma, you can't. Ice will be so fucking pissed if you show up there. It's club business; you can't get in the middle of it. You know the rules."

"Honey, I really appreciate the rules and all, and I've done everything I can to abide by them. But now I have my child to worry about. That rattlesnake on the front porch changed the rules for me. I'm going somewhere where I'll feel safe. I'm going to the one man that grounds me. The only man that makes me feel truly protected. If that pisses him off, then so be it."

"You shouldn't travel alone. What if this person follows you?"

"I'm not traveling alone."

"Who's going with you?" I ask curiously.

"Ari."

"What?! Not only will Ice be pissed that you have flown to Ireland, he will be furious that you brought Ari along as well!"

"I don't think you hear me. I don't care. I'm leaving and that's final."

"Then I'm going, too!"

"Like hell you are!"

"You can't stop me! If it is ok for Ari to go, then I see no reason why I can't go."

"What the fuck, Honey? This isn't a party. This isn't a girl's trip to Europe."

"I know that! I'm not stupid, Emma. But you're going to need all the help you can get if this person follows you. It's better to have reinforcements. It's better to have Ari and me!"

She gives me a disgusted look and says in defeat, "I'm not gonna win this argument, am I?"

"Nope!"

"Fine. And I suppose I am paying for the tickets as well," she teases.

"Well ... I was kinda hoping that you would offer."

She shakes her head. "I'll get the tickets booked. Hopefully, we can be on a flight in a day or two. Make sure you're ready to go." She pauses and then adds, "And Honey, not a word about this to Hawk or any of the boys."

"You're not going to tell him?" *Oh fuck, I can't wait to see her pull this one off.*

"Absolutely not. He would lock us up before he would let us leave. Not a word!"

"My lips are sealed," I say as I turn to leave. *Guess I've got some packing to do.*

"And Honey?"

I turn back. "Yes?"

"Have a good time on your date tonight."

"You think I should still go?" I ask.

"Absolutely. Everything should continue as normal. Nothing should alarm Hawk or any of them that we're up to something. Got it?"

"Yep, I got it," I say and turn and leave the room.

It's 6:30 pm and I am ready to go. Emma helped me get ready and if I have to say so myself, I look damn good. Hawk should be here any minute and I am just sitting in my room nervous as hell waiting for him.

A few minutes later, Emma comes up and says, "Hawk is here."

"Oh fuck."

"Honey, stop. You are gonna have a great time." She pauses and then adds, "Now stop worrying and get your ass downstairs. Your big bad biker awaits."

I laugh and make my way to the door. Taking one last glance at myself in the mirror, I turn and walk out. *Here goes.*

I come down the stairs and find Hawk pacing. I have to giggle; he's nervous too. It's not like this is a blind date, but we are both acting like it. When he catches a glimpse of me coming down the stairs, he says, "Look at you. You look beautiful," and walks over and kisses me on the cheek.

"Thank you. You're looking pretty good yourself," I say.

He smiles and says, "Ready to go?"

"As ready as I'll ever be." I glance back at Emma and she's beaming. It's comical, she's acting like a mom sending her daughter on her first date. I turn back and follow Hawk out of the house.

Instead of his bike, Hawk has the club SUV. We get in and he heads toward Erie.

"So, where are we going?" I ask.

"Mi Scuzi." He pauses and then adds, "Is that ok?"

"Of course." Mi Scuzi is one of the top restaurants in Erie; it's almost impossible to get a reservation. "How did you get a reservation so quickly?"

"Being the VP of a biker club has its privileges." He laughs and I join in.

Once we get to the restaurant the maître d' escorts us to our table. It's in a quiet corner and very romantic. We sit and Hawk says, "I hope this is alright."

"Will you stop? Everything is perfect, Hawk," I reply.

We have a wonderful dinner; they serve some of the most amazing food I have ever eaten. Once the initial awkwardness passes, we fall into easy conversation and things seem a bit more normal. He mentions something about going out again on Sunday and before I answer, I realize that I'm gonna be in Ireland on Sunday. But, obviously, I can't tell him that, so I lie and say, "That would be wonderful."

When we leave, we get in the car and he says, "So, what else would you like to do?"

I laugh. I have a feeling I know what he's hoping for, but frankly, I don't know if I am ready. And, since we are leaving tomorrow, I know that I have packing to do. "Would you mind taking me back to the house?" Seeing the disappointment on his face, I add, "I'm kinda tired." I feel bad, but I can't tell him why. I'm a little annoyed with Emma right now, because her plan to leave tomorrow is fucking with my date, but in a way, I understand too.

"Sure, Honey. There's always Sunday," he replies.

"Yes, there is," I say encouragingly.

CHAPTER 20

The next day, from Gate 24 of Buffalo Niagara International Airport, Emma makes a call to Hawk. I never thought she would be able to pull this off, but son of a bitch, she did.

I can hear Hawk yelling through the phone. Then Emma replies, "I'm calling to tell you that Honey, Ari, and I are safe. We're in Buffalo at the airport, about to board a plane." Then there is more yelling from Hawk, and then Emma says, "We're going to Ireland." And some more yelling. "Sorry, Hawk, but that's not gonna happen." She pauses then adds, "I love you—really, I do. And I know you're doing everything to keep me safe. But you have a club to run and Ice is counting on you."

The yelling seems to have subsided and Emma is listening. Then she replies, "No, he is not. I'll make sure of that. This decision was mine and mine alone. I can't put you all in danger again. Not after all the turmoil you all went through because of me in the last few weeks. That rattlesnake was the last straw. Anyone could've been bitten. I'm not taking any more chances. I'll be safe in Ireland and I'll be with Caden. I need him, Hawk. Once he finds out about all the threats he will be glad that I'm with him and not here where he can't protect me."

She's quiet again and then looks at both Ari and me. "My initial plan was to go alone. It's a long story, but they both insisted that they go with me. They really didn't give me much of a choice,"

Just then, I hear over the intercom, "This is the final boarding call for Aer Lingus flight 3784 to Belfast. All passengers, please board immediately."

Emma says, "Hawk, I need to go. They just announced the final boarding call for our flight."

I tug on her arm and say, "Let me talk to him."

"Hang on, Honey wants to talk to you." She hands me the phone.

"Hey," I say into the phone.

"Have you lost your ever-loving mind? You know better, Honey," he yells.

"Yes, I know better," I reply.

"I swear you fucking girls are gonna be the death of me yet. You're gonna give me a fucking heart attack. Is that what you want?"

"Hawk baby, calm down. I'll look after them. No worries. I've got this."

He finally stops yelling and says, "If you say so. Doesn't look I have much of a choice in the matter, now does it? Put Emma back on." I hand Emma her phone back and say, "He's better now."

She takes the phone and says, "Hawk, we really need to go. I'll let you know when we get to Belfast."

She listens for a minute and says, "I will," then disconnects the line.

She looks over at Ari and me and says, "That went well," and we all bust out laughing as we proceed to board our plane.

We get ourselves settled on the plane. Emma purchased first class tickets and I have to say, it's really nice. I've never been on a plane before and I'm a little nervous, but I don't tell the girls that. I've always been the one to ground both of them and I refuse to let them know that I'm a little scared right now. Emma is sitting next to me by the window and Ari is in the middle section of the plane across the aisle from me. Once everyone is on the plane, they close the door and a few minutes later, the plane begins to move away from the gate. *Here goes...*

Taking off is a rush. The thought of something so big lifting off the ground and flying into the air amazes me. Part of me wishes I had the window seat so I could watch, but the part of me that is still a little shaky about flying is glad that I am sitting on the aisle. Once we reach our cruising altitude—I only know that terminology because the pilot just announced it—Emma takes out a book and begins to read. I brought a book too, so I reach under the seat in front of me to get my backpack and pull my book out as well. Ari gets a set of headphones from the flight attendant and starts watching a movie. The screen is in the back of the seat in front of her, so it's like she has her own personal movie theater right there. It's really cool.

The flight is long but direct. We're offered food, snacks, and drinks. Alcohol is free in first class and it takes everything in me not to order a drink. Lord knows I want to. But my sobriety is important to me, so I don't. Eventually, I fall asleep and I don't wake up until the plane is about to land. My nerves come back as the plane touches down on the ground, but thankfully we land safely.

We go through the process of customs, getting our bags, and hailing a cab. This part is definitely not fun, but obviously, it is something that all international travelers must go through.

It's pretty late when we finally get to Rebel's family's home. We approach the door and Emma knocks. I'm sure we're going to wake up the whole house. A few seconds go by and nobody answers. Emma knocks again and then we hear yelling from inside the house. *Holy crap. What the fuck is going on?*

The door finally opens and we see Rebel standing there shirtless and barefoot, wearing only a pair of sweatpants that hang low on his hips. But his state of undress is not what concerns me, it's the sexy redhead standing in the middle of the living room wearing nothing but a pair of black lace panties. We all just stand there in shock and then Emma says, "Rebel? What's going on here?" Poor Ari looks like she is about to cry and frankly, I can't say that I blame her.

I can't believe that Rebel has allowed himself to get into a situation like this. He's a smart guy and to cheat on Ice's sister right in front of him would be a death wish. Surely he knows that. But I've seen him get himself into sticky situations in the past and it wouldn't surprise me if this is exactly what it looks like. The fact that Rebel is tongue-tied and remains silent just makes him look more guilty.

"Ari ..." Rebel says loud enough for all of us to hear. Silence deafens the room, then Rebel finally yells, "Ciara, I fucking said to go back to bed! Now!"

The half-naked girl who I assume is Ciara looks from Rebel to Ari with a pout. "Fine!" she stammers. As she stomps up the stairs, she yells, "Good luck explaining this one!" Her laughter fills the silence in the room.

Rebel watches her go and then turns back toward us. "What are you girls doing here?" he asks as he gestures for us to come in.

We walk through the door silently, bags in hand. It's very awkward and Rebel hasn't started explaining yet, which is making the whole situation worse. Emma says as we walk into the house, "Maybe first you should explain what we walked in on."

Rebel looks at Ari apologetically and says, "Babe, it's not what it looks like, I swear. I never touched her."

Ari doesn't say a word, but her eyes begin to well up with tears.

"Honey, maybe you and I should step outside and let these two have some privacy," Emma says.

"No!" Ari states. "Stay here and hear what he's got to say. Then, Emma, you can tell my brother all about it," she threatens.

Rebel flinches at her words, then reaches for Ari's arm and pulls her over to the couch. "Sit," he says. "There's no need to involve Ice in this. Just let me explain."

As she sits down, she looks at her watch and says, "We've been here long enough. You can start explaining any time, Rebel. I'm not going anywhere." She crosses her arms and adds, "Yet!"

Emma and I do what Ari says and sit down. Finally, Rebel begins to explain, "Today, we finally got a lead on my mam and da. I was pumped, anxious, and unable to sleep. So, I came downstairs to get something to eat. Ciara came down after me."

"Why is she even here in the middle of the night?" Ari asks.

"She is dating my brother, Damon. I assume she was in his room."

Ari seems to accept that reply and silently gestures for Rebel to go on. He says, "She came down half-naked and tried to get me to take her back to my room, but I refused. I never touched her and I didn't instigate this." He says pleadingly, "I swear!"

He waits for Ari to say something, but she remains quiet, apparently in deep thought. Then he adds, "Babe, do you really think I'd be so stupid to do something like this with your brother upstairs? He'd fucking kill me!"

Ari still doesn't say a word, but I think his last words make sense to her. I mean really, Rebel isn't suicidal.

Emma watches her curiously and when Ari doesn't say anything to Rebel, Emma says, "Ari? I believe he's telling the truth. If there's only one thing he's said tonight that makes perfect sense and totally backs up his story, it's the fact that he wouldn't be stupid enough to do this with Caden in the house."

She looks at Emma and finally speaks, acting as if Rebel wasn't even in the room. "But how do you know, Emma? How do I know I can trust him?" she asks.

"Has he ever given you any reason, ever, to mistrust him?" Emma asks.

"No."

"And do you think he would be stupid enough to take the risk?"

"No," she says as she looks over at him.

"Then I think you have your answer. You need to give him the benefit of the doubt and not make assumptions about things that didn't happen."

Still looking at Rebel and crying silent tears, she says nothing. He pulls her into his arms and says, "Babe, I love you. I would never do anything to fuck up what we have. Ever."

"I love you too, Rebel," she says, hugging him back.

They hug for a few more minutes and then Rebel says, "So what the hell, ladies? What're you doing here?"

I laugh and say, "That's a long story." I pause and then add, "I'll let Emma tell you." *I'm not taking the flack for this one. This move was all her. Even though she pulled it off brilliantly, it's all on her.*

Emma rolls her eyes at me. Before Emma can explain, we hear someone coming down the stairs.

"What the fuck is all the noise about?"

It's Ice. Let the fireworks begin. I laugh to myself. When he gets to the bottom of the steps, we see that he is also wearing nothing but a pair of sweatpants that hang low on his hips. *Holy fuck!* My mouth begins to water and then I remember my place. I may not be able to touch, but nobody can stop me from looking.

"Fuck, Emma!" he says when he sees us.

"Hey, Cade," she says with all the confidence in the world. I actually expect "surprise!" to come out of her mouth next. I'm just waiting for him to blow up at her—at all of us, for that matter. But he totally surprises me. He walks over to Emma and carefully pulls her up from the chair. His arm wraps around her waist as he pulls her in close.

He leans in like he's going to kiss her. But instead, he says, "I'm not gonna ask why you're here. I'm not gonna ask why you've pulled my sister out of school and brought her with you. I'm not gonna ask why you didn't give me so much as a notice that you were coming. But if I wasn't so fucking happy to see you right now, I would put you over my knee and spank your ass!" He leans in and kisses her.

Hot damn!

When the kiss is over he turns to Rebel and asks, "Did you know about this?"

"No! I'm just as surprised as you," Rebel replies.

"You can say that again," Ari says. At her words, everyone busts out laughing. That is, everyone but Caden, who just looks confused.

He turns back toward Emma and asks, "What the fuck is so funny?"

Smiling, she says, "I'll fill you in later. It's a long story."

"Fine, so tell me why the fuck you're here. Did something happen?"

"Another long story," she replies.

"Well, is someone going to tell me what the fuck is going on here?" he says and I can feel his anger rising.

Emma plays him perfectly and evades his questions. "Babe, I'm really tired. Can we go to bed now? I'll tell you everything, just not here." He nods grudgingly, seeming to be placated for a while. She then turns toward Rebel and asks, "Do you have room for us?"

"Of course," Rebel replies. "Emma, you're in with Ice, of course. Honey, your room is the first one at the top of the stairs, to the right."

Ice walks over and grabs Emma's bags as well as my own, and then starts to head for the stairs. Rebel grabs Ari's and does the same. As he walks up the stairs, Caden says, "It's been a long day and I'm sure you girls are tired. Let's go to bed; we can talk in the morning."

CHAPTER 21

Emma and I get up early and it's not long before Ari joins us. We are in the kitchen rummaging through cabinets and such trying to put together some form of breakfast. There's nothing like making ourselves at home.

A few minutes later, Ice walks into the kitchen and says, "Ladies."

"Ice," Emma and I say in unison. Emma turns toward him and hands him a cup of coffee.

"Thanks, love," he says, kissing her on the cheek.

Just then, Rebel comes in. Ice looks at him and asks, "All good?"

"Yes, they'll be here first thing in the morning," he replies.

"Good," Ice replies.

"What will be here?" Emma asks.

"Need to know, babe, remember?" he tells her and she sighs in frustration. One of these days, she'll get it.

Doc and Ryder join us in the kitchen and Ice says, "I'm gonna go call Willie." I have no idea what he is talking about and I know he isn't gonna tell us, so I just continue to go about getting breakfast ready for everyone.

Not long after Ice leaves the kitchen, Ciara, the chick from last night, comes in. I can tell already that this chick is a player; if someone doesn't set her straight soon, she is gonna cause all kinds of havoc. I appoint myself and just as I'm about to bitch-slap her, Ice comes back into the kitchen. He looks around and he sees the problem.

Just as smooth as ever, he walks over to Ari and kisses her on the cheek. "Hey, sweetheart," he says.

She gives him a big hug and says, "Hey, Caden."

He then turns to Ciara and says, "Ciara, I don't believe you've met my sister."

She stutters, "N...No ... I haven't. Not formally, that is."

"Imagine my surprise when Rebel here, my Sgt. at Arms, asked my permission to date my sister. But, as I'm sure you well know, Rebel isn't just my sergeant, right? He's my friend and cousin on my dad's side. We bikers, we like to keep it all in the family, now don't we, Reb?"

Smirking, Rebel replies, "Absolutely, Boss!"

"And you wanna know something else about us bikers?" he asks.

"Yeah, what?" she says defiantly.

She is as dumb as a fucking box of rocks. She still doesn't get it. But I'm sure that she is about to.

"We don't take kindly to bitchy ex-girlfriends fucking around with our old ladies. You got me?" When she doesn't answer, he gestures over to Emma and says, "This is Emma, my old lady. And over there is Honey, the woman who single-handedly takes care of all my boys."

"Nice to meet you," she says curtly. She then turns and stomps out of the kitchen. And just like that, she is gone.

Then Ice turns to Rebel and says, "Liam just came down. Let's go." Rebel nods and they both leave the kitchen. They aren't gone long before we hear them all proceed down the basement. They must be having a meeting.

About forty-five minutes later, we have everything ready for breakfast. Emma walks over to the basement door, opens it, and calls down to the boys,

"Breakfast is ready."

We set up everything buffet style to accommodate everyone. The guys come up and the first in the room is Rebel. He beelines straight for Ari, gives her a big hug and whispers something in her ear that I could not hear. She giggles, so it must have been something good. He then turns to Emma and me and says, "Thanks for making breakfast, ladies. I'm starving!"

"Plates and utensils are over there." I point to the end of the counter. "And food is over there," I say, pointing to the table in the center of the room. "Help yourself and find a place to eat," I say as the rest of the guys begin to pile in the kitchen.

Once everyone has food and is scattered around the living room and dining room eating, Ciara walks in. She's wearing a pair of skinny jeans that look as if they've been painted on her body. She has a Harley shirt on, the front is covered with sparkles and displays the Harley logo but the back is cut out, revealing that she is not wearing a bra. *This little bitch is about to get sent packing.*

"Where's my breakfast?" she asks petulantly.

"All the food is in the kitchen. Help yourself. We cook, we're not serving," Emma says, and then she leans over to Ice and asks, "What's her deal?"

He laughs again and says, "Another long story."

Everyone seems to enjoy breakfast and Damon and Patrick don't seem too annoyed that we took over their kitchen. The girls and I clean up the food and dishes while the guys chill out in the living room. When we're done, we join them.

The guys talk for a while. Liam, the man that I assume has been helping them, excuses himself, saying that he's got some things to take care of. After he leaves, Ice says, "That reminds me, I need to make a few calls myself." He turns to Emma and says, "Sorry, babe. Let me get this taken care of and then we can discuss those notes." He looks over at the guys and says, "When I'm done, let's meet downstairs."

"You got it, boss," Rebel says.

Cade leaves the room and heads out the front door while the rest of us continue to hang out and catch up.

CHAPTER 22

About fifteen minutes later, Ice comes back into the house and says, "Let's get to the bottom of these notes." Emma begins to speaks and he adds,

"Let's take this discussion downstairs." He looks at Emma and says, "You and Honey come, too."

Once we get downstairs, everyone grabs a seat at the table. He says to his brothers, "So, I bet you all are wondering why the girls are here."

Doc speaks up and says, "Well, the thought did cross my mind, but I wasn't gonna ask." He laughs. "Not my business, man," he adds.

"Me too," says Ryder. "I figured that was between you and your old lady."

"Well, for the record, it's not a thing between me and my old lady, Ryder. This is more pressing and fucking serious, so cut the laughter."

"What's up, boss?" Doc asks, the smile disappearing from his face.

"Well, it appears that we have another situation back home: threatening notes and a fucking stalker. This guy—I assume it's a guy—is after her as well as me. My first thoughts go directly to Grayson, but ... shit, I don't know. I have nothing on this."

He continues, "I want to call Hawk and get his take on this, but I also want you all here when I do. Who knows, maybe he's gotten more info since the girls left the States." He turns toward Emma and says, "But before we call Hawk, why don't you get the boys up to speed on what you know?"

She nods and proceeds to tell them about the threats, the rose, and the rattlesnake.

"Fuck, Emma! A rattlesnake? Did anyone get hurt?" Rebel asks.

"No, luckily we heard the snake before it was able to bite anyone. Spike shot it."

"You got anything else, sweetheart?" he asks. "Maybe something that you might have overlooked?"

She shakes her head. "No, that's everything that I know."

"Ok, I'm calling Hawk now."

He dials and the phone starts ringing. He sets it down on the table and puts it on speaker—after three rings, Hawk answers. "Ice, man, listen before you say anything. You need to know that I had no fucking idea that she was going to Ireland. She left no clue until she was at the airport boarding a flight. I couldn't stop her, man. I tried, but I found out about her leaving too late. I'm sorry. I fucked up."

I can't help but laugh. It's a quiet laugh because I don't want to be disruptive, but ... the poor guy. He's beside himself over this. Suddenly, I feel bad for him and hate that he is so upset. Hopefully, Ice won't come down on him too harshly.

"Hawk, stop." Hawk keeps talking and finally, Ice has to speak over the top of him, "Hawk, I know. It's ok."

"What?" he says. Another giggle escapes me.

"Emma told me everything. It's ok," he says, then adds, "I've got the girls, Rebel, Doc, and Ryder here. You're on speaker." He waits for him to say something, but he doesn't, so Ice keeps on going. "Emma filled the boys in on everything that she knows up to the point when she left the States. You got anything to add? Anything happen since?"

"Possibly. I've had Dbag doing some digging and I think we might have an idea who's doing this."

We're all expecting him to continue, but when he doesn't Ice prods him along. "And?"

"My initial gut feeling told me that this had something to do with Grayson. So I had Dbag poke around Grayson's aunt first since he lived with her. Then I had him look into the Graysons themselves, the family who adopted him."

"Anything?"

"It looks like Mark isn't their only kid. They adopted three other children—two boys older than Mark and a younger girl. Both adoptions happened after Mark was adopted."

"So, he has siblings. Do you really think they could be involved in this?" Ice asks.

"Not these siblings."

"He has others?"

"Well, I believe that the Grayson family is clean. But, if you remember, he spent his earliest years with his mother's sister. She couldn't keep him and after a year put him up for adoption."

"Yeah, I remember that. So?"

"Well, Aunt Jenny did give up Grayson. But she kept his brother."

"His brother?" Ice asks incredulously. It is clear that he is completely blown away by this news. Fuck, I think we all are. By the expression on her face, I don't even think Emma knew Grayson had a brother.

"Yep, Mark had a brother. A biological brother."

"How do you know they are biological brothers? Maybe Aunt Jenny had another drug addict sister who had kids," Ice says.

"That could be the case, but I seriously doubt it," he replies.

"Why?"

"He's a twin."

"A what?"

"A twin."

Ice looks at Emma. "Did you know anything about this?" he asks.

"No," she says, astounded.

Yep, I was right. She had no fucking clue.

"So which one did I kill?" he asks, worried.

"The right one?" Hawk says. "Hell, I don't know, Ice. This is so fucked up."

"So you think that this twin is the one terrorizing Emma?"

"It makes sense," Hawk replies.

"Where does he live?"

"Upstate New York. I'm sending a few guys up there today to check things out."

"You got a name?"

"Yeah, Joe Russo."

"Ok, good work, Hawk. Keep me up to date on what you find out."

"I will."

"Anything else going on that I need to know about?"

"Nothing earth-shattering, but things are moving along here. Brianne is out of detox and awake. I've had Spike detailed to her room and I've been checking on her daily. Doctors say she will be heading to rehab in a day or two."

Emma jumps in and says, "Hawk, please ask them to wait to send her until I can get home. I really need to see her."

"I'll see what I can do, Emma, but I can't make any promises."

"Anything else?" Ice asks.

"Clubhouse renovations are moving along. And I met with Gypsy yesterday. Everything's going as scheduled with the Satans. What about you guys? Any luck with Rebel's parents?"

"Yeah, we finally got a lead. If all goes well we should be home day after tomorrow. If anything changes, I'll let you know."

"Sounds good."

"I'll wait to hear back from you about the brother," Ice says.

"Will do, boss. Talk to you soon."

He disconnects the call and looks around the room. "Any thoughts?"

Nobody says a word for the longest time. Then, Emma breaks the silence. "It all makes sense now," she says as if she is talking to herself.

"What, babe? What makes sense now?"

"Mark. There was always an uncertainty that I felt about him. I could never pinpoint the reason why I was never able to set a date for the wedding. I always thought it was because of you, but at the time, I never believed that you would be back in my life. It's the question that's always plagued me about him and it's all so clear to me now," she says. When nobody responds to her words, she continues, "Mark was always odd. One minute he would be this sweet guy and then the next minute he would seem very aloof and detached. He truly scared me during those times, but I always chalked it up to him having a bad day. There were so many times when I almost believed he was two different people. I thought I was losing my mind. Now I know he was two different people, and both of them messed with my head." She gets up from the table.

Ice shakes his head and says in almost a whisper, "What a fucking asshole." He walks over to Emma and pulls her into his arms, "You ok, babe?" He pauses then adds, "We'll get him. I promise."

"I know," she says. "I know."

He really does love her. I can see it in his face, the way he speaks to her and his actions. I guess I always knew it, but seeing them interact like this, it's staring me in the face.

He turns back toward the group. "I think we're done here. Unless anyone else has anything to say? We've done everything we can on the Grayson thing. It's now a waiting game until we hear back from Hawk. And everything is ready for Friday. So, I think you all deserve a break. What do you think?"

"A break?" Rebel asks.

"What do you mean, a break?" Ryder chimes in. "You never give us a break when we're working on shit." He laughs.

"I do too!" he says defensively.

"Yeah, boss, sure you do," Doc says sarcastically.

"Well, if you all don't want a break ..." he teases.

"No, no, we do. Really, we do!" Ryder says quickly.

"That's better! Now, what I was saying is that you all have been going 24/7. But now everything is in place and we don't need to do anything until Friday. So, if you want to take in the city, do it. If you want to go hang with Declan at our sister club, do it. Take the next 36-odd hours and do what you want to do." Everyone still looks shocked; I think he may have just lost his mind. "What?" Ice asks. "Can't I give you fuckers a day off?"

"Well, Ice," Doc says, "in all the years you have been our prez, you have never given us a day off."

"Of course I have."

"Name one," he retorts.

"Well, there was the time when ... ok, so maybe the time when ... oh, fuck it. Never mind. Just take the fucking day off."

They all start laughing. He turns to Emma, who is laughing right along with us, and says, "You too?"

"Well ..." she says sheepishly, "you have to admit, it's kinda funny."

"Fuck it, you fuckers can do what you want. My girl and I are gonna do some sightseeing. If anyone wants to join us, feel free." He pauses and says, "Babe, get on the web and check out the sights. Let me know where you want to go. The day is yours."

Every one of them gets up from the table and hurries out of the room. We can hear Ice laughing as we leave.

CHAPTER 23

Later that day, after getting myself settled, I go back downstairs and enter the living room. Everyone is talking about going somewhere and I want to go, too. *I think.*

"Go where?" I ask.

"We're gonna do some sightseeing. Wanna come?" Emma says.

"Sure, where're we going?"

"Rebel, can we go?" Ari asks.

"Fucking stop! You all are making me fucking dizzy," Ice says and we all stop talking and look at him. "This is what's gonna happen. Emma and I are going sightseeing tomorrow—Giant's Causeway, Game of Thrones tour, and a night on the town in Belfast. Today, we're hitting the Harley store so she can get appropriate riding attire. Anyone who wants to go, be ready in thirty minutes."

Thirty minutes later, we all leave for the Harley store. Emma gets a pair of boots, a sweater, and a jacket. Ari gets herself some boots. I, of course, already have everything I need, so I can actually save some money. But of course, I never miss an opportunity to go to the Harley store. You never know what might be new that I have to have. After shopping, we all grab some lunch and then return back to the house around four. We spend the rest of the evening just hanging out.

The next day the sightseeing begins. We leave right after breakfast and spend the whole day enjoying the sights. Ireland is a beautiful country and even though we are here for some rather unpleasant circumstances, I'm so glad that I came.

The next morning, Ice and the boys spend most of the day in the basement. He says that we need to be ready to go back to the States today and that Damon and Patrick will be taking us to the airport later tonight. I'm not so sure about Damon and Patrick. There's something fishy about those two...frankly, I don't trust them.

We get our stuff together so that we are ready to leave and then we spend the rest of the day keeping ourselves busy. Emma and I are reading some smutty romance novels and Ari is totally occupied with her phone, probably on Facebook. I can't concentrate on the book. I'm worried about the guys and what's about to happen. I get up several times and pace. Emma tries to reassure me, but it's not working. I just have an uneasy feeling about everything and I can't shake it.

The boys come up from the basement late in the afternoon and start to get their stuff together to leave Ireland. They're all loaded up with weapons, they look like a fucking swat team. When it's time for them to leave, Ice comes over to us with a guy that none of us have met yet. He says, "Emma, this is Reese. He will be staying with you and will make sure that you all get to the airport on time tonight."

"Oh," she replies, surprised. "I thought Damon and Patrick were taking us?"

"They are, Reese is just insurance. I really don't completely trust those two and although I felt I needed to give them something to do to keep them out of my hair, I also had to make sure that the task I gave them got done." He smiles.

I knew there was a reason not to trust those two.

"I get it," Emma replies.

Ice leans in and kisses her on the cheek and says, "We've gotta go, babe. I'll see you at the airport." He kisses her on the lips this time and turns to leave.

"Caden?" she calls after him. He turns and raises an eyebrow. "Please be safe. Come back to me in one piece, please," she says and I can see she is just as worried as I am.

He walks back over to Emma and gives her another hug. "Do you really think you can get rid of me that easily? I'll be back, I promise." He kisses her again and then proceeds to hug Ari and me.

"See you later, Emma," Rebel says as he gives her a hug. Doc and Ryder both say their goodbyes as well and they all head out the door, accompanied by Liam.

At first, we try to keep busy. We're all so worried about the boys and we know that if we just sit around the house doing nothing, our worries will get the best of us and make us crazy. We have a couple of hours before Damon and Patrick take us to the airfield and since all our stuff is already packed and ready to go, we decide to watch a movie. Nothing passes time better than a good movie.

The waiting is killing me.

"Damon, would it be ok if we headed over to the airfield now?" Emma asks. "I don't mind waiting there and I am sure the girls don't either."

"I don't," I reply.

"I'd love to go now," Ari adds.

Damon looks over at Patrick and says, "It's a little early, but what do ya say bro? Wanna head over to the airfield? It might give us some extra time to take care of that other matter."

Patrick gives Damon a knowing look and nods. "Ok ladies, we'll get your stuff loaded in the SUV."

After all our bags are loaded, we all get in the car and head out. None of us have any idea of what to expect, all that we know for sure is that we're going to an airfield.

Forty minutes later, we arrive at the airfield. There isn't much there, just a building and a couple of runways for the transport flights that go in and out of this facility. Ice said that our flight would be leaving at midnight. I look at my watch; we have three hours to wait.

"Well, Emma, Patrick and I need to go. Will you girls be alright?" Damon asks Emma shortly after we arrive.

Surprised that he is just gonna leave us here, she says, "You're not staying until the boys get here?"

"We can't. We have something that we need to take care of." He pauses for a moment and then adds, "But you ladies have Reese. Isn't that why Ice had him tag along in the first place?"

I knew these assholes were gonna bail on us. Ice did too, that's exactly why he had Reese.

Damon says, "It was nice meeting you girls. Have a safe flight home."

Patrick adds, "Yes, really great to meet you all."

And just like that, they are both walking out the door and we're now left alone with Reese in a strange airfield.

As the time ticks by, the more worried and concerned we become. Ice made it perfectly clear to us that we were to get on that flight whether he and the boys made it or not. As it gets closer to midnight, I begin to worry.

At 11:30, the pilot and co-pilot greet us.

"You ladies with Caden Jackson?"

"Yes," Emma replies.

Looking around, the pilot asks, "He here?"

"No, not yet."

"And you are?" he asks.

"Emma, I'm his fiancée."

"Is there a way you can contact him? I was told that we would be transporting four women and five men. By my count, we're a lass and five lads short."

"We're waiting on the other six. They're supposed to be here by now."

"You realize, ma'am, that I can't wait for them. I need to have this plane loaded and boarded by midnight," the pilot says.

"I know. We still have some time. Hopefully, they'll get here."

At 11:45 Emma's phone rings. She looks at the caller ID and breathes a sigh of relief. She quickly answers the phone.

"Caden, where are you?" she says frantically into the phone. I can't hear what he's saying and I am silently praying that they are on their way. Then she says, "I already did and he said that he's on a tight schedule. He says the plane doors have to be closed promptly at midnight." Again silence. Then she adds, "Are you driving?"

She listens some more and then she cries, "Oh God, Caden! You sure he's gonna be alright?"

Oh, fuck, what's happened?

Emma calms down and then replies, "Ok. Did you get your aunt and uncle?" She doesn't say much more and then disconnects the line.

"So what happened?" I ask. I can't take the wait any longer.

"They're almost here. But something has happened." She looks at Ari, who is looking at her with concern. "Rebel got shot. He's ok for now and Doc thinks he's gonna be fine, but Caden wanted me to prepare you."

"Oh, Emma. He has to be ok," she says and begins to cry. We both try to comfort her, but I know she won't rest easy until she sees him.

About ten minutes later as we are boarding the plane, I see a van speeding down the airfield road toward the main entrance. It turns down the last corner and heads straight for our plane. "That has got to be them," I say, pointing in its direction. Emma and Ari look up hopefully.

The van pulls up to the plane steps and the driver slams on the brakes.

Ice jumps out of the van and opens up the back. Ryder and Doc come around back and the three of them maneuver Rebel from the van and proceed to carry him up to the plane as we run ahead and get out of their way. A couple follows them, and I assume they are Rebel's parents.

When Ice gets to the top of the stairs, the pilot greets him. "You must be Ice."

"Yeah, that's me. Where can I put him?"

"Over here." After everyone is on the plane, he says, "We'll be taking off in a few minutes. You all might want to find a seat and strap in."

Ice gets Rebel situated and he wakes up. I can't make out what they are saying, but I'm sure that the fact that he is conscious is a good thing. I need a little me time, so I take a seat toward the back of the plane, pull out my book and read. I'm hoping that once we take off, I will fall asleep and we can leave this nightmare.

CHAPTER 24

A jolt and a screeching noise wake me up. Getting my bearings straight, I look around and realize that I'm still on the plane. From what I gather, we've just landed. *Thank God we're back in the States. I never thought I would be glad to be home.*

Once we deplane and get our bags and such, Hawk meets us at the airfield to take us back to Edinboro. When we get back, we all proceed inside the house, the boys following carrying Rebel. They take him straight to Ari's room and lay him on the bed. He is really holding his own; I am surprised that he hasn't passed out yet. He's looked better though, and I can't help but worry about him.

Caden turns toward Doc and Ryder and says, "You boys look beat. We've done all we can here and you need to get some rest. There's shit we have to deal with tomorrow and I want everyone fresh." They nod in unison, say goodnight to everyone, and leave.

Hawk looks at his watch and says, "Brewer should be here in ten minutes." Caden nods and they both go out to get the rest of the bags. Ari remains with Rebel. When Hawk comes back in he takes my bags up to my room. When he comes back down he gives me a hug and says, "I'm so fucking glad you're home."

I smile at him and reply, "Me too."

Brewer shows up not long after and Ice takes him to Rebel. I decide that maybe I should put something together for everyone to snack on. I think it's gonna be a long night. As I am rummaging through cabinets, trying to scrounge up what I can find, Emma walks in. "Whatcha doing?" she asks.

"Oh, just making some coffee and getting some snacks together. It wasn't like we flew commercial and were fed on the plane. I'm sure everyone is probably famished."

"Good idea. Can I help?"

"Yeah, why don't you get coffee cups, cream, and sugar? I'll cut up some cheese and we can make a cold cut plate for folks to snack on."

"Sounds good." As we're working on getting things together, Ari walks into the kitchen.

"How's Rebel?" I ask.

"He'll be ok, I think. The doctor is with him now. Brewer says he's really lucky. From what he can tell, the bullet exited through Rebel's abdomen cleanly without hitting any major organs. He's concerned about the blood loss but says that it is manageable. He said he'll give me a more accurate update once he fully examines him." She's completely exhausted, poor thing. I bet she didn't get any sleep on the flight.

She plops herself down onto one of the bar stools. "Is that coffee done yet?"

"Almost, sweetie," I reply. Ari lays her head down on the counter.

"Ari, you really should go get some sleep," Emma says.

"I know, I will. I just want to wait until Brewer is done examining Rebel. I won't be able to sleep until I know for sure that he's going to be ok."

When the coffee is done, Ari gets her cup and goes back to her room to check on Rebel. Emma and I bring the serving pot, cups, and snacks into the family room. Aillise and Connor, Rebel's parents, appear grateful as they both pour themselves a cup. I've not spoken with either of them and right now, I'm not sure that I want to. I'm finding it hard to believe that they sent their son away and I don't understand their reasons. But it looks like they are gonna be around for a while, so I guess I need to make nice.

A few minutes later, Ice and Brewer come down from Ari's room. "Now that my sister is out of earshot, give it to me straight, Brewer. How is he, really?" Ice asks.

"Ice, he's been shot. He's in pain and he's lost some blood. From what I can tell from the exit wound and the bleeding, it doesn't appear that the bullet hit any vital organs. But, and I know that you're not gonna like this, I'd really like to get him over to the hospital to make sure he doesn't have any internal bleeding, just to make sure."

"Damn it, you know how I feel about hospitals. It's a gunshot wound. They'll have to report it and there's no way they can know that he was in Ireland when it happened."

He thinks for a moment and then says, "If I promise to keep it under the radar, will you bring him in?"

"Can you guarantee no police report?"

After thinking about it, he replies, "Not 100%, but 95%?"

"I don't know if I can risk that 5%, Brewer."

"So you're willing to risk his life instead," he replies dryly.

"You're not playing fucking fair!"

"I'm just telling you like it is. I would rather see you be safe than sorry. I know how important he is to you, hell, how important all your brothers are. So, are you willing to take that 5% risk or are you gonna risk his life?"

"Well, if you put it that way, I guess I really don't have much of a choice, now do I?" I know that Ice hates to be backed into a corner and that's exactly what Brewer is doing. But on the other hand, we're talking about Rebel's life.

"Let me make the arrangements and you can bring him in tomorrow." Brewer pauses and starts putting things back into his bag. "I think my work here is done for now. Doc did a great job getting the bleeding to stop, so I'm not too concerned there. He's a little pale, but I don't think the blood loss is dangerous. I gave him some pretty potent pain meds, he'll sleep the rest of the night. But someone should keep an eye on him."

"I think that is covered. I don't see Ari leaving his side tonight."

"Yeah, I think you're right."

"Thank you. I really appreciate you coming over here this late."

"You'll get my bill!" he says, laughing. He starts to walk out of the room and Ice follows him to the door. He says, "I'll call you and let you know when to bring him to the hospital for that MRI."

"You got it." Ice opens the door and thanks him again as he leaves.

"Hospital?" Hawk asks. He walks over to Ice and lowers his voice. "Are you sure about this?"

"I know what you're thinking. But we don't have a choice. Brewer knows how we feel about hospitals and gunshot wounds, but he insisted. And frankly, I don't want to take any fucking chances with Rebel's life."

Hawk nods. "I agree, but are you ready to face the consequences of this?"

"Brewer assures me that he'll do everything he can to keep Rebel's visit under the radar. I've gotta trust him."

"Yeah, I know."

We hang out for a little while before it becomes clear that everyone is running out of steam. Turning to Emma, Ice says, "Babe, do you want to let everyone know where they'll be sleeping tonight?"

"Sure," she replies sweetly. She says, "Aillise and Conner, you will take the first room on the left. Honey, you will keep your room, and Ari, since Rebel is already in your room, I am assuming that you will want to stay with him."

"Yes, thanks, Emma," Ari replies.

"Hold on one minute," Ice says firmly. "Ari is not sleeping with Rebel."

I knew he would have something to say about that.

Emma turns toward him and says, "Babe, remember what you said earlier about being happy with whatever plan I had come up with?"

"But ..." he grumbles, but she quickly interrupts.

"She'll be fine. I don't think her virtue is in any danger tonight. Remember, he's in there because he's recovering from a gunshot wound."

Ice grumbles again and clears his throat. "Well, when you put it that way, I guess it's ok." I'm proud of Ice for letting it go. Emma sure knows how to reel him in. He then looks over to Rebel's parents and says, "Do you need anything?"

"No, Caden, your lovely girl here has taken care of all of that. She got us what we needed for tonight, as long as you don't mind Connor wearing your clothes. The rest we can get in the morning."

"Good. We'll take you out tomorrow to pick up whatever you may need." Turning toward Emma, he says, "Thanks, babe." She smiles and helps Ari and me clean up the plates and cups.

"Well, if you all will excuse us, I think we're going to call it a night," Connor says.

"Sleep well—and if I didn't say it before, I'm glad you both are safe.

I know I got a little defensive with you on the flight. I guess we have a lot to talk about," Ice says.

"Yeah, I guess we do," Aillise says.

"We'll talk more about where we go from here in the morning."

They nod and Aillise says, "Goodnight, Caden."

"Goodnight."

Ice walks into the kitchen just as we're finishing up and says, "You ladies are fantastic."

"I think I am going to turn in," Ari says.

"Goodnight, sweetheart. Let us know if Rebel needs anything," he says, kissing the top of her head.

"I will."

"Me too," I say. "I'm beat." I make my way out of the kitchen and up to my room. Before I get too far the doorbell rings. Ice walks over to answer the door. *Who could be stopping by at this time of night?*

Sgt. Briggs walks inside Ice's house, followed by two other men. One is a uniformed officer and the other is Joe Russo, Grayson's twin. He's the man that has been threatening Emma and the reason why we left Edinboro and went to Ireland.

I don't run from Sgt. Briggs anymore. It's a relief that he knows everything now, but I still can't fight the ache that I feel every time I see him. My heart hurts for everything that we've lost, as well as the fact that I know he'll never forgive me for all that I have done. I deserve that...but it doesn't make it any easier to swallow.

I can see the disgust on Ice's face. The general camaraderie in the house suddenly stops as Emma walks over to Ice. She gasps at the resemblance that Joe Russo has to Mark Grayson and she reaches for Ice's arm for support.

"Hello, Emma," Russo says. Emma's hand tightens on Ice's arm and she begins to tremble. Russo says, "Good to see you again." He winks at her and it makes my skin crawl. This sick fuck did a number on Emma by switching places with his brother. That explains why she had said that there were times when it felt like she was dating two different men. What sick bastards.

Briggs steps close to Ice and whispers something in his ear, and then louder so that everyone can hear, he says, "Caden Jackson, you are under arrest for the murder of Mark Grayson. You have the right to remain silent. Anything you say can and will be used against you in a court of law. You have the right to an attorney. If you cannot afford an attorney, one will be provided for you. Do you understand your rights as I have read them to you?"

"Caden!" Emma screams. "No!" She pulls his arm away as Briggs tries to place him in handcuffs. When her efforts don't work in her favor, she throws her arms around him and begins to cry hysterically. "You can't take him!"

Hawk walks over to her and pulls her off him. "It's ok, baby," Ice says. He looks directly at Hawk and says, "Call the Vitalis and get Sainte here."

I recognize the Vitali name, but who is Sainte? Hawk nods as if he knows exactly what needs to be done. He always does.

Ice turns back toward Emma and says, "Everything's gonna be alright, darl'n. Take care of our kid. I love you both."

"Caden! No!" Emma cries again. Hawk tries to settle her down, but it's really not working.

"Caden, do you understand?" Briggs repeats.

"Yes," he replies. Briggs nods and walks him to the door. Emma continues to scream hysterically, which isn't good for her or the baby.

I silently watch this whole thing play out. Emma breaks down as they take the man she loves away in handcuffs. We all know that he's being arrested for murder. We also know that he committed said murder, for her.

My blood begins to boil. Suddenly the hard face of jealousy emerges and all the hate and anger from when she first arrived resurfaces. Everything was perfect before she came along. I had Ice and we were happy. Never in a million years did I think he had some long-lost girlfriend that would come back into his life and ruin everything he and I had together.

But she did. And even though I have grown to like Emma, I can't control this jealousy when it rears its ugly head. As I hear the car drive off into the night, I make a vow to myself. If Ice ends up spending the rest of his life in jail, friendship be damned, I'll never forgive her.

Why did things have to change? When I came to this club, Ice took me in, gave me a place to live and a job. He was my savior and I loved him for it. I still love him. Hell, I'll always love him. Probably not in the way I did then, at least I don't think so. I'm moving on, but I just can't turn those feelings off. I'm loyal to the core, and when someone fucks with someone I love, I don't take it too well.

I wish I had known that this was gonna happen. Hell, I should have known. I should have prevented it. But, nothing, absolutely nothing could have prepared me for this – even if I had known.

I'll never forgive her for this. If he ends up doing real time for this, I swear I will make her worst nightmare seem like a happy place.

CHAPTER 25

Present day

It's been two days since Ice got arrested. We are all still in a state of shock; none of us expected this to happen. I find myself wondering when things will get better. Haven't we been through enough?

I can't look at Emma with any kindness right now. All my rage is directed at her. This is her fault. My stomach turns when I think of Ice sitting in jail because of her.

Hawk has been busy the last couple of days; other than him passing through here and there, I hardly see him. I know that he's contacted Vitali and Ice's legal counsel is arriving today. I also know that he had new identities made for Rebel's parents and thankfully, they are leaving. It's all been hush-hush as to where they are going, which I assume is for their own good.

Before Hawk left this morning, he mentioned to me that we will be having company for dinner. Apparently, Ice's lawyer and Sainte are coming. I'm really not in the mood for entertaining, but he asked me to prepare something nice for them tonight and so I am in the kitchen busily preparing my best Italian meal. I thought it would be fitting since we were entertaining the Italian Mafia.

I remember when Ice got arrested he told Hawk to call Vitali and asked him to get Sainte here. I assumed then that he wanted

Michael Vitali for his legal connections. The club has used them in the past. But I had no idea who Sainte was. When I asked Hawk about him, he was very vague. He said something about him being a top button pusher for the Vitali crime family. I had no idea what he meant, so I asked him what a button was and he said, "When Michael Vitali tells him to push a button, Sainte pushes the button." He didn't elaborate and I can only guess that the button is a reference to someone's life. So Sainte is a mafia hitman.

The whole idea of them being involved in this makes me nervous. I've never really had any dealings with the Mafia before, but I've heard stories. The last thing I want is for us to get into a situation where we owe them something. When I voiced my concerns to Hawk, he quickly assured me that our relationship with the Vitalis is good and that I don't need to worry. Obviously, he couldn't tell me more.

It's now half past six, and dinner is just about ready. Emma, who has spent the last two days in her room, finally decides to come down. Ari has taken food up to her a time or two but she just picks at it, which is a great fucking way to take care of Ice's kid. I understand that she is upset, but she has a little one to think about. It's not always all about her. I told myself that if she didn't come down for dinner tonight and actually eat something, I was going to go up there and force-feed her.

"Hey Emma, nice of you to join us," I say sarcastically.

"Hi Honey," she says and sits down on one of the barstools. When I don't pay her any mind, she adds, "I'm sorry for being such a pain the last couple of days."

"Don't worry about it, Emma. We're all under a lot of stress. Ice getting arrested is not a good thing for this club, but we're dealing." I don't want to come right out and say it, but I want her to understand the ramifications of all this. I want her to see that this is all her fault.

"I know, and I know I'm responsible."

There it is. Well, at least she fucking admits it. I have to say, I fully expected her to place blame elsewhere.

She continues, "Hawk tells me that I shouldn't feel responsible, but I do."

What. The. Fuck! How dare he tell her that when he knows as well as I do that if she wasn't here, we would still be back in our old clubhouse and safe. Hawk and I are definitely having words later.

"You know what, Emma? I'm not in the greatest of moods right now and I'm afraid that I will say something that I shouldn't. Let's just drop this and concentrate on dinner. We've got the Vitalis coming soon; they should be here any minute."

"But Honey, I feel that there is tension between us and I want to clear the air."

I hold up my hand and take a deep breath. "Yes, there is tension, but I am not going to do this now. Grow a pair, Emma, and be the old lady that Ice needs you to be." She stares at me, offended. *Poor, pitiful Emma. I'm so done with this shit. I'm sick of everyone coddling her and I'll be damned if I continue to do so.*

Before she can respond, the front door opens and in walks Hawk and two very handsome men. One is dressed in a suit and I am assuming he is the lawyer. But the other one ... *holy fuck!* He's dressed in tight jeans and a black t-shirt that fits so perfectly that you can see the ribbing of every muscle on his torso. His jet-black hair is cut in a short buzz that totally accents his chiseled face. He looks like a man that nobody would want to run into in a dark alley.

Hawk walks into the kitchens and says, "Ladies, this is Vince Bonito and Nick Saintero," as he points to each man respectively. "Gentlemen, this is Emma, Ice's old lady, and Honey, my old lady."

Old lady? When did that happen? Did I miss a conversation we had?

I notice that Nick—or I guess he goes by Sainte—looks at Emma curiously. He walks over to her and says, "It's a pleasure to finally meet you, Emma. I've heard a lot about you from Ice."

What the hell does that mean? And why would Ice be talking to this guy about Emma?

He then turns to me. "And Honey," he says as he winks and takes my hand and kisses the back of it, "truly a pleasure."

Who the fuck does this guy think he is? I quickly look over at Hawk—he looks annoyed, but he doesn't say anything.

The other guy, Vince, speaks up and says, "Hello ladies, I'm Ice's attorney. It's a pleasure to meet you both."

Sainte is still watching Emma closely, and I can't make out why. Is it an attraction? What the fuck? Surely this guy knows that Emma belongs to Ice, especially if Ice has talked to him about her. The irritation riles me and I can't take it anymore. "Ahh, Mr. Saintero," I say, "why don't you put your eyes back in your head? Emma is taken." Everyone in the room looks at me and I can see that they are surprised by my outburst. I don't care, I may not like Emma right now, but she still belongs to Ice.

"Well listen to you, Miss Feisty Pants," he says and begins to laugh. "I've been called many things, and most of them are true. I've never been called Mr. Saintero. Call me Sainte."

"Well, whatever you call yourself, Emma is off-limits." I turn and walk back into the kitchen, calling behind me, "Dinner will be ready in five minutes."

How dare he call me feisty pants? I don't know what it is about this guy, but he totally rubs me the wrong way.

A few minutes later, we sit down to dinner. When asked about Ice's case, Vince proceeds to tell us that he met with Ice before coming here and after talking over the details of the case, he's hopeful. He also mentions that Sainte will be staying on for a while at Ice's request, and that he will be Emma's personal bodyguard while Ice is away.

Why the fuck does she need a bodyguard? I don't trust this guy. At least we have some good news about Ice. Hopefully, he will be coming home soon.

After dinner, Vince and Sainte linger for a bit and then Vince leaves. I guess when they said that Sainte would be staying on, they meant that he would be staying here. Tonight, he will have to sleep on the couch, as Rebel's parents are not leaving until tomorrow. I guess he can have that room after they leave. This house is getting to be more and more like a fucking hotel.

When Hawk gets ready to leave, I follow him out. When we get to his bike, I ask, "So when did I become your old lady?"

He chuckles. "The day you agreed to go out with me."

"It's that simple?"

"It's that simple, babe." He gets on his bike and says, "Honey, I'm counting on you to make Sainte comfortable."

"Why is he here?"

"Now don't you go worrying about that. Ice has his reasons."

"But Hawk, there's something about that guy that I don't trust."

"You're being ridiculous. Ice trusts him with Emma's life. That's testimony enough for me that he's a good guy."

"But ..."

"Honey, it's all good. I promise," he says. "I gotta go." He kisses me goodbye and then puts on his helmet. He waves and pulls out of the driveway.

I still don't trust Sainte. That fucker called me feisty pants.

CHAPTER 26

I storm back into the house. Emma, Ari, and Rebel have already gone to bed and Sainte is sitting on the couch. Obviously, the asshole is waiting for me to make up his bed. Well, that ain't gonna happen. I stomp upstairs, grab a blanket, pillow, and sheet from the linen closet and make my way back down. I throw the bedding on the couch and say, "Here," then proceed to walk off.

"You don't like me, do you?" he says.

I stop and turn back toward him. "Well, if you really want to know, no, I don't."

"I think you're being unfair. You just met me." He pauses and then says, "Are you always this judgmental of people you've just met?"

"Judgmental? You think I'm judgmental?" I step up closer to him and get in his face. "Listen, asshole, I saw the way you acted with Emma. I've got your number, buddy, and I'll be damned if you're going to fuck with her or Ice that way."

"Oooh, you're a little spitfire aren't you?" he says and I know he's making fun of me again.

"You really think that you're something, don't you?"

Before I can finish my thought, he moves in close and backs me against the railing of the stairs, our bodies touching. He says, "Oh baby, I know that I am. And before you know it, you're gonna be dreaming about me in ways that not even you can imagine."

"Fuck you!" I spit, then push him away and proceed up the stairs.

"Goodnight, Feisty Pants," he says and begins laughing.

I call back downstairs, "Don't call me Feisty Pants!" *He may be easy on the eyes, but he's still an asshole.*

I get to my room and I'm fuming. *What a cocky son of a bitch! How dare he assume that I would dream about him? What a dick!*

The next morning, I come downstairs and hear laughter coming from the kitchen. When I get to the kitchen, I find Emma and Sainte laughing. They stop when they see me come in. I head straight for the coffee. A few minutes go by and Sainte says, "So you've never been to the Presque Isle?"

"Nope. Can you believe it? I've lived here all my life," Emma replies.

"Well darling, we need to fix that," Sainte says. "How about we go Saturday afternoon? It's supposed to be a nice day."

Emma giggles and says, "Oh, I would love that!"

What the fuck? "I thought you were going to visit Ice on Saturday?" I interrupt. Sainte pisses me off already, but Emma's reaction to him is making me mad as hell.

She glares at me and says, "I am, but that is Saturday morning. My afternoon is free."

"Wanna join us, Feisty Pants?" Sainte asks.

Fuck! The last thing I want to do is spend an afternoon at Presque Isle with this asshole, but I'm conflicted because I feel that I need to keep an eye on these two. I really don't know what's gotten into Emma. A day ago she was depressed and distraught about Ice. Now she is like a different person, all happy and smiling. How she has allowed this smooth operator to charm her is beyond me. I say reluctantly, "Yeah, I will join you." I pause, then add, "I told you last night, don't fucking call me Feisty Pants!"

Sainte just laughs and Emma says, "Oh Honey, lighten up. Sainte doesn't mean any harm. He just likes getting a rise out of you and you deliver every time."

Fuck you, Emma! Fuck all of you! I storm out of the kitchen and go back upstairs to my room.

As I leave the kitchen, I hear Sainte say, "She's something!" Emma laughs.

A few minutes later, there is a knock at my door. I open the door and it's Emma. "Got a minute?" she asks.

"What?" I say shortly.

"What's going on with you, Honey?"

"What do you mean?" I reply defensively.

"I've never seen you act this way before."

"I don't know what you're talking about."

"Honey, you've always been the nice one, the welcoming one. Why are you being so mean to Sainte? He's only here to help," she says.

"Emma, you are so fucking blind. You are being sucked in by his charms and you'll be sorry. He's planning on causing problems for you and Ice, and if you don't stop it now, it's gonna be too late."

"That's ridiculous. Ice is the one who asked him to come here." She pauses and then says, "What makes you think that he's trouble?"

"Emma, I've been around the block a time or two. I've seen his kind a million times. They come in all good-looking and charming, and then they set their sights on something they want. Nothing, and I mean nothing, will stop them from getting it ... and they don't give a shit who they have to destroy in the process. And Emma dear, he fucking wants you!"

Emma laughs heartily. It's almost comical how hard she is laughing. "Oh Honey, I'm surprised at you." She pauses and then says, "For the short time that I have known you I've always thought that you were sharp and your instincts were right on. But sweetie, you are so wrong on this one." She pauses again and then says, "Because the one that he's set his sights on, is you, darling!" And before I can utter another word, she turns and leaves the room.

No way! Absolutely not! Everything he does, he does to piss me off. Why in the hell would she think the opposite? And even if

Emma is right, it's obvious that I'm taken. I'm Hawk's old lady and definitely not available.

The next day Emma and Sainte leave early for the jail to visit Ice. Ari and Rebel leave not long after them to get some air, or so Ari says. I assume that Rebel just wanted to get out of the house now that he's feeling better; I'm sure they wanted some alone time.

So it's almost lunchtime and it's just me alone in the house. I have to say, I am enjoying the quiet too much. Sainte in my face all the time is getting old already; I will be glad when he goes back to New York. Ice can't get released soon enough. I hear the rumble of a Harley long before I see it pull into the drive. Looking out the window, I see that it's Hawk. *Well, isn't this a nice surprise.*

A few minutes later he comes in the front door and says, "Hey doll, whatcha doing?"

"Enjoying the peace and quiet," I reply and laugh. "It's nice having the house to myself."

"I bet. It's beginning to look like Grand Central Station around here."

"Tell me about it."

He laughs and says, "So, I had a break this afternoon and thought I would spend it with my best gal. Interested?"

I smile and say, "I would love that."

"We're going on my bike, darl'n, so you better change."

"Ok, be right back." I run upstairs to change. I love surprises like this and am looking forward to an afternoon alone with Hawk. A few minutes later, I'm dressed in my full riding gear, which consists of jeans, boots, and a jacket. I'm carrying my helmet in my hand and I've already put my gloves on.

"Damn, you are one hot biker chick," he says and comes forward and kisses me full on the mouth. He takes my breath away and then he steps away, leaving me hanging. "Come on," he says as he heads for the door.

Something is up. Hawk is definitely not a spur of the moment kind of guy. He's got something planned. But what?

We get on his bike and take off. We drive for a while, just cruising through the back roads and enjoying the nice day. After about an hour of just riding, Hawk heads back toward town and we end up at his place. When he stops the bike, I dismount from the bike and he follows. Hanging out helmets on the handlebars, we proceed to his front door.

When we get inside, he seems nervous but doesn't say anything at first. Then he says, "So, I thought you and I could use some alone time." He pauses as if hesitant and then says, "Is that ok?"

I stand there for a moment and think about what he is asking. *Am I ready for this?* I ask myself, and right before I'm about to say yes, two images pop into my head—Ice and Sainte. *What the fuck? No, I'm not going there. It's time to move on with my life and my future is with Hawk. End of story.* "Yes, it's perfect," I say.

Hawk wraps his arms around me and buries his face in my neck. His warmth seeps into my skin and his strong arms surround me. There is definitely chemistry between us, and it pulses through my body with a fierceness.

He leans down and kisses me, softly at first, and his kiss gradually becomes more urgent. My legs go weak as his tongue tangles with mine. The intensity of his kiss leaves me breathless and wanting more. I reach for the edges of his cut and drag it off his shoulders. I then reach for his shirt and start to lift it up. Yes, I want this. I not only want this, I need this. It's been a long time since I've been with a man. He releases my lips and takes a step back. Suddenly, I felt cold and alone. I ask, "What's wrong?"

The love this man has for me is written all over his face. I can also see his lust. He wants me just as much as I want him. So what's the problem?

"Let's take this upstairs," he says.

I nod and he growls, pulling me to him, claiming my lips again. The slow, demanding way he takes my mouth to his makes me cling to him like a starved kitten clawing for food. Before I know it he is lifting me into his arms and carrying me up the stairs, never breaking our kiss.

When we get to his bedroom, I drop down onto my knees and start to fumble with the fly of his jeans impatiently. I want his cock badly. He helps me by sliding his jeans down just far enough for me to get to the prize. He looks so damn sexy standing there with his pants partially down his legs.

Once his cock is free, I take it in both hands, gently running my hands up and down his shaft as I look up at him. I lick the little notch on the underside of the head, moving my tongue rapidly against him.

"Honey!" he growls, letting me know how good I'm making him feel. I'm glad. This man has stood behind me from the beginning. He's always been there for me and it makes me feel good that I can give him something back.

He reaches down and tangles his fingers in my hair, urging me to go on. He doesn't have to coax me at all. I gladly wrap my mouth around his cock, sucking him in as deep as I can, taking his tip to the back of my throat. I work my tongue all over his dick as he moans in pleasure. My left hand rests on his balls, alternately rolling and gripping them. His cock gets harder in my mouth and he starts moving his hips toward me a little with each stroke. He grasps at my hair a little tighter. Looking up at him, I see that his eyes are fixated on the pleasure I'm giving him. I am now the one with the power and this big strong biker is at my mercy. The feeling is intoxicating.

Before I know it, he lifts me from under my arms. In one fell swoop he turns me around and now I'm standing next to the bed, my back to his front. Hawk reaches around and undoes my jeans and slowly slides them and my panties down over my hips, allowing them to hover at my knees. He bends me over the bed and his cock swiftly enters me from behind. *Holy fuck, it feels so fucking good.* He growls again when he's completely sheathed inside me and pumps me hard. He's so deep inside me it feels like my insides are about to explode. He maintains a hard, steady rhythm and before I know it I detonate into one of the most amazing orgasms I've ever had. It doesn't take long after for Hawk to reach his orgasm, and he grunts and groans as he releases himself inside me. *Holy fuck! I needed that.*

We clean ourselves up and get dressed, then as Hawk comes over toward me, he says, "Thank you, baby. You are amazing."

I smile at him coyly and say, "Thank you, I aim to please."

CHAPTER 27

Rebel's parents are gone now, but Sainte refuses to sleep in the vacant bedroom. He insists on still sleeping on the couch. He's been here three days and it's only gotten worse. I've been having trouble sleeping at night and tonight is no different. I decide to go downstairs and get something to drink. When I get to the bottom of the stairs, the house is dark. *Good, he's asleep.* It's always a plus when I don't have to interact with him.

I quietly make my way into the kitchen. Opening the fridge, I see that there is an open bottle of sparkling grape juice. What I really want is a glass of wine, but this is the next best thing. I take it out and proceed to the cupboard to get a wine glass, because using a wine glass makes me feel as if I am really drinking the good stuff. Just as I'm pouring my juice, a voice in the darkness startles me. I spill it everywhere as I jump.

"So what's your story, Feisty Pants?" Sainte asks.

I ignore him as I clean up my mess. Then I turn and face him. *Fuck!* He's standing there in a pair of black sleep pants that hang low on his hips and he's not fucking wearing a shirt. He's ripped, and he's got a tat on his left shoulder that comes down over onto his pec. I can't quite make out what it is in the dark, but it's intriguing. My eyes take in his body and I have no words. He really is fucking beautiful. It's a shame his personality doesn't match his looks.

"Well?" he prods.

"That is none of your business," I reply.

"Oh come on Honey, I know you've got a story." He moves in closer to me and says, "What's the matter, Feisty Pants? You afraid of what I might think of you when you tell me?"

"You know what, Sainte? You're a cocky ass. I'm not afraid of anything and frankly, I don't give a shit what you think of me." I grab my glass of fake wine and start to walk away.

Before I get too far, he grabs my arm and pulls me back. Taking the glass of out of my hand, he begins to back me against the kitchen counter. He sets the glass down and leans in close. His body is right up against mine and I can feel his erection pushing into my core. My body betrays my mind and I can feel the wetness pool between my legs. "Look, darling, you may think that you hate me—hell, right now, you probably do—but that doesn't stop you from wanting me." He pauses and leans in to whisper in my ear and says, "And even though you hate me, it doesn't stop me from wanting to tear your clothes off and fuck you into oblivion."

Oh my. I thought the chemistry between Hawk and I was strong, but it's nothing compared to what I feel with this guy ... which only makes me hate him more.

I'm breathless from his words and his close proximity and before I can utter a word, he pulls me into his arms and kisses me, hard and possessively. Everything in me fights to not kiss him back, but I can't. My arms reach up around his neck and I greedily kiss him back. My body melts into his. The kiss seems to last forever and when he breaks the kiss and steps away from me, I feel cold and bereft. "Told ya," he says smugly and suddenly I remember that I hate him. Before he sees it coming, I reach up and slap him hard across the face.

"Don't fucking touch me again!" I spit. As I storm out of the kitchen, I can hear him laughing behind me. *How dare he laugh at me!*

I get back up to my room, without my grape juice I might add, and I am even less tired than I was before. I'm fuming mad. *Why the fuck did I fall into his trap? Why did I let him get the better of me? Fuck! I've known guys like him all my life. I know the signs of an asshole, and he fits the bill perfectly. Then why? Why the fuck did I let him kiss me, and more importantly, why did I kiss him back?*

That kiss. Oh my ... No man, not even Ice, has kissed me like that. It wasn't a kiss of just passion or lust. No, it was a kiss of dominance, power, and complete control. He fucking owned me during that kiss, devouring my mind as well as my lips. And I fucking let him!

I was definitely right about him. He's trouble. I can't let this happen again; if I do, he will destroy me.

As I lie in bed, I can't stop thinking about the feel of his lips or how his body felt pressed up against mine. And then, reality takes a front row seat, and I think about Hawk. He's always been there for me and this is how I repay him, by kissing another man.

I need to tell him. I have lied to him about so many things, mainly for his own good and to not hurt him, but I can't keep this from him. First, it's the right thing to do, and second, I don't trust Sainte to keep his mouth shut about it. Hawk is safe. He's strong and grounded. He won't hurt me. And he's who I need to be with. I'll tell him tomorrow.

As I finally start to fall asleep, I have one last thought.

I'm so screwed.

The next morning, I'm stalling. I've been in my room much longer than normal; frankly, I'm afraid to go downstairs and face Sainte. But I have learned over the years to not run from my fears, so I take one last look at myself in the mirror and decide that I have to do this. I can't hide here forever, or until he leaves. When I walk down the stairs, I find him and Emma sitting together on the couch watching a movie. I can feel my blood pressure rise when I see that she is sitting so close to him. If I didn't know better, I'd swear they were snuggling. *What the fuck?*

That's when I decide that Ice needs to know what's going on. I grab my purse and keys and head for the door.

"Where are you going, Feisty Pants?" Sainte asks.

Without turning around, I say, "Out," and slam the door behind me.

I get in my car, slamming that door as well. I am so mad I could spit nails. *How dare she do this to Ice? Doesn't she get what he's done for her? Doesn't she understand that he's in jail because of her? And Sainte! He's supposed to be Ice's friend. Ice trusts him and he should respect their friendship. And he was fucking kissing me last night!*

I get to the prison and register as a visitor. They say that it will take a few minutes and tell me to have a seat. I sit down in the outer lobby and wait. I can feel my heart hammering through my chest. My blood pressure must be through the roof. Finally, an officer comes out and says, "Miss Benson, follow me please."

I follow him through a doorway and down a long hallway. He takes me into a room, but it's not like a visitation room. There is a woman in the room and he says, "Officer Chapel needs to pat you down."

I nod and the woman takes me behind a screen and gives me the standard pat-down. Then she says, "She's good." He nods and walks out the door and I assume that I'm supposed to follow him.

He then takes me into another room that is small, consisting only of a table and three chairs—two at the table and one by the door. "Wait here," he says and leaves the room, closing the door behind him. A few minutes later the door opens back up and in walks Ice, followed by a different security guard. Relief washes over me. It's so good to see him, even if they have him wearing an orange jumpsuit and handcuffs. I smile and he smiles back. The guard says, "Fifteen minutes, Jackson, then you go back."

Ice nods and the guard parks himself in the chair beside the door.

Ice sits down, placing his cuffed hands on the table. He says, "Honey, what are you doing here?"

"What? Not happy to see me?" I tease.

"Of course I am, but when they told me I had a visitor you were the last person I expected to see. Something happen?"

"No, not yet. But if you don't step in and nip it in the bud, something will."

"What's going on?" he asks.

"Ice, look, I know you've got your reasons about having Sainte here, but I'm telling you, he's bad news. You need to send him packing before he ruins everything."

"Honey, I can't do that. I've known Sainte for years and I trust him, just like I trust all my brothers. He's here for a reason and he needs to stay."

"Ice, you don't get it. He's moving in on Emma, and she's letting him!" I say in a furious whisper. The last thing I want is for the security guard by the door to know our business.

And to my surprise, Ice laughs. Not a chuckle, but a wholehearted laugh.

"Stop laughing, Ice, this isn't funny. He's fucking with your woman. You need to stop it!"

He stops laughing, but I can still see the mirth in his eyes. His amusement is really pissing me off; the situation is not funny! He reaches for my hand, but before he touches me, the guard says, "No touching." Ice quickly rescinds the gesture and looks at me apologetically.

"Honey, darling. When have I not known what I was doing?"

"Well, I guess as long as I've known you ... never," I say.

"Exactly." He pauses. "I have my reasons for having Sainte here. Trust me when I say that I have nothing to worry about where Emma is concerned."

"But you don't see them," I plead. "They're always together. Always laughing together and this morning, I swear they were snuggling on the couch."

He laughs again and says, "I don't have to see them. You've always trusted me; you have to trust me now. I promise, there is nothing to worry about."

"But ..."

He shakes his head. "No buts. Just trust me."

"Ok." I put my head down. *Why do I feel like I was just scolded?* Shaking these feelings away, I ask, "So how are they treating you?"

He laughs again. "Good. I get three meals a day and roof over my head."

"That's not what I meant." I roll my eyes.

"It's ok. The food sucks and I sure as hell miss your cooking, but other than that and being away from home, it's all good."

"I hate seeing you in here in that god-awful orange jumpsuit."

"What, orange isn't my color?" he teases.

"Are you gonna get out of here soon?"

"Vince is hopeful, but we don't know anything for sure."

The guard interrupts, "Two minutes."

"Well, I better go. I'm sorry if I stepped out of line, Ice. I was just worried for you."

"I know. You've always looked out for me and it means a lot."

He smiles and then turns to the guard and says, "I'm ready." The guard gets up and walks over to him. When he gets behind him, Ice stands up and turns toward the door. He looks back at me and says, "Thanks for coming by. It's good seeing you." He pauses and then adds, "Remember your promise."

And suddenly I remember. Right before he left for Ireland, he asked me to look after Emma for him. I thought I was.

"Bye, Ice. Take care of yourself," I say as the tears begin to well up into my eyes. Him being here fucking sucks. I hate it and it breaks my heart that he can't be home with his family. *Damn you, Emma.*

Right after he leaves, the guard who brought me to this room comes to the door. "Miss Benson, I'll escort you out."

I nod and get up from the chair. We leave the same way we came in and he walks me all the way to the door. *Well, that accomplished nothing.* I can't help the way I feel and I still think that he is being too trusting of Sainte. I don't care what Ice says, I'm not gonna let them out of my sight.

CHAPTER 28

When I get back to the house, Emma and Sainte are gone. *Where did they go?* I wonder, and then I remember that today is the day that they were going to Presque Isle. *Wasn't I supposed to go with them? Yes, I was. They fucking left without me.* All my anger floods back as I walk into the kitchen and throw my purse on the table. I can only imagine what they have been up to this afternoon.

"Whoa there darling, calm down," Hawk says from the doorway.

"Oh fuck! I didn't think anyone was home. You scared the shit out of me!" *When did he get here?*

He walks over and gives me a kiss on the cheek and says, "Sorry, love. I was in Ice's office getting some paperwork on the new clubhouse."

"Oh," I say.

"So what's got you all upset and where have you been?"

I hesitate at first, but then I remember that I promised myself that I would be honest with him. "I went to see Ice," I say.

"You did?"

"Yes."

"Can I ask why?" He's quite calm and it surprises me. I expected him to yell or something, but nothing.

"I wanted to talk to him about Sainte and Emma," I say.

"Honey, I told you to mind your own business where those two are concerned. Ice trusts him, therefore I trust him."

"But Hawk, you didn't see them this morning. They were snuggling on the fucking couch. I'm telling you, she's cheating on him!"

"Honey, Emma is not cheating on Ice."

"What makes you so sure?"

"Because I know Emma. She would never cheat on him."

Why can't he see what's right in front of his eyes? Why can't he see that this guy is bad news? Am I the only sane one around here? I shake my head. "Why won't you listen to me?"

"I am listening to you. I'm just telling you that you're wrong." He pauses and then asks, "Tell me, what did Ice say when you told him this?"

I look down at the floor. "He said he trusted Sainte and Emma, and that he had his reasons for having him here and that he stays."

"See? You shouldn't worry."

"But Hawk, they are always together and laughing together. You haven't seen it, but I see it all the time."

"Drop it, Honey."

"Drop it. Just like that, I'm supposed to drop it when I see that one of my dearest friends is getting screwed over."

"Dearest friend, is that what he is now?"

"Don't you dare! Don't you dare turn this on me, Hawk! We've discussed my relationship with Ice at great length. He's a friend and nothing more."

"Then it must be Sainte."

"What?" I ask, shocked.

"If it's not Ice that you want, then it must be Sainte."

"That's not true," I say defensively. But I immediately remember the kiss and I can feel my face flush. *Fuck, he's gonna see right through me.* My conscience quickly reminds me that I was going to tell him everything, but after that comment, I don't know if I can.

"Ok, if it's not true, then explain to me why seeing them together gets your panties in a twist."

"Because I believe they are hurting a friend."

"And that's it?"

"Yes."

"Well, let's nip this in the bud right now. You don't have to worry about Ice getting hurt anymore. I don't want to hear about this again."

"But ..."

"No, Honey, this conversation is over." He grabs his keys and walks out.

Well, shit! That went well. Frustrated, I stomp upstairs. *Why can't they see that this guy is up to no good like I do?*

I spend most of the day in my room until I hear the front door closing. *They're home. Maybe I should just give them both a piece of my mind and be done with it. Yeah, that's what I need to do.* I leave my room and make my way down there stairs. I'm a woman on a mission—I'm gonna set them both straight. Yeah, you know what they say about the best-laid plans. I get to the bottom of the steps and the most adorable ball of fur greets me. *Oh. My. God. Emma got a puppy.* I can't resist. My anger completely dissipates as I stoop down and scoop the little guy (or girl) into my arms. "Oh my goodness, who are you?" I say to the pup, purposely ignoring Emma and Sainte.

"This is Hobbes! Isn't he the cutest?" Emma reaches over and pets the pup lovingly.

Now I have to acknowledge her. "Is he your dog?" I ask.

"Yes! Caden and I have been talking about getting a dog for a while now—well, since I found out I was pregnant—and so today, we got him!"

"Don't you think that should have been something that you and Ice did together?" I say. I can't hide my annoyance at the fact that she did this without him. I'm still holding Hobbes and I swear if he licks me one more time I am going to turn to mush and I won't care what Emma and Sainte have done.

190

"Oh, we went to see Caden first, and he insisted that we go and pick out a dog. He didn't want me to wait until he got out." She pauses and then says, "He said that you stopped by this morning."

"I did," I reply shortly. *I'll be damned if I elaborate on that. What I went to see him about is none of her fucking business.* I put the dog down and quickly change the subject, saying, "So what kind of dog is it?"

"He's an Alaskan Malamute, thirteen weeks old. I've been in contact with the Wolf Spirit Sled Dog rescue for a while now. I had been planning on getting a dog even before I found Caden again. Not long before I came to the club, they took in an expectant Mal mom and I have been just waiting for the pups to be born and to be ready for adoption. Nikki called this morning and said I could have the first pick of the litter. So when I told Caden about it, he couldn't refuse. He also knew I had been waiting."

"So he's gonna be big?" I ask.

"Yes, hopefully huge!" she says, laughing.

Through this whole conversation, Sainte has been watching me curiously. I hate the way he stares at me and I'm terrified that he's gonna spill about the kiss. Oddly enough, he doesn't utter a word. But his eyes on me are unnerving.

CHAPTER 29

The next couple of days are pure hell for me. I try my hardest to heed Ice and Hawk's words, but seeing Emma and Sainte together makes me totally insane. *I know I'm right about this; I just need to show Ice and Hawk so they will believe me.* I've thought about going back to see Ice, but since it went so well the first time, I decide not to. I just don't know how to stop the train wreck that is about to happen.

My phone buzzes and I look down and see that it is Hawk. We haven't spoken much the last couple of days, ever since he yelled at me. I was hoping that after our "lunch" together that he would stay here with me or invite me to his place to stay, but he hasn't. "Hey there," I answer.

"Hey, Honey," he says into the phone.

Wow, I don't even get a babe. He's still mad at me. Part of me understands why, but fuck, it's not like I cheated on him or something.

Ok, I did, but he doesn't know that. Suddenly I feel like shit. I've been lying to him and I promised myself that I would not do that.

Just as I'm about to say something, he adds, "Vince is back in town. Got in late last night. I know he's been down at the jail most of the morning and he has a meeting with the District Attorney who is prosecuting Ice's case this afternoon. I've invited him over for dinner."

Well shit, he doesn't even ask. "Ok, of course." I pause and then add, "Will you be joining us as well?"

"Yeah. I have a feeling that he's got big news, so I'm inviting some of the other club members too."

"Ok. I'll have to run to the store, but I'll make sure we have something nice."

"Send Sainte," he says.

"But what about Emma?" I ask.

"Fuck, have him take her with him," he says and then adds, "I gotta run. See you tonight?"

He's softened a little, which gives me hope that his anger has subsided. "Yep, I'll do you proud," I say.

"You always do, babe. You always do," he says and then disconnects the line.

I make my way down to the kitchen to see what I have and what I need. *What the hell should I make?* It's still early, so I hadn't even given dinner a thought yet. When I get to the kitchen, Sainte is rummaging through the fridge. "Looking for something?" I say coldly.

"Yeah. Are we outta beer?" he asks.

"Isn't it a little early for beer?" I ask.

"Feisty Pants, it's never too early for an ice-cold beer," he says smoothly.

I think it's his cockiness that angers me more than anything. Yes, he's gorgeous, but so is Ice, and he's not half as cocky as Sainte. But he's not Ice! my subconscious quickly reminds me. *No, he definitely is not.* As I stare at him, my cheeks flush as memories of our kiss fill my head. I quickly turn away from him and say, "I'm just getting a grocery list together. I'll be sure to add beer. Any particular kind?" *Holy shit, why am I being nice to him?*

"Something dark would be good," he says.

I nod. "Hawk called a few minutes ago and said that Vince is back in town. Said he's coming for dinner tonight and that I should send you to the store if I need anything." I really hate asking him to do something for me, but Hawk and I both know that I don't have time to grocery shop and prepare dinner too.

"Sure, Feisty Pants. Anything for the woman that kisses like a cat in heat," he says, and now I know my cheeks are flushed. I immediately look around the kitchen to see if anyone heard and realize that we are alone. He adds, "Don't worry, your secret is still safe. Emma is upstairs napping and Ari and Rebel are down at the lake." He moves in close and says, "You got me all to yourself, babe." He pauses and then says, "So, how 'bout it?"

I quickly push him away and say, "Fuck you! That kiss was a momentary lapse in judgment. I will never kiss you again." When he stands there without saying a word, I continue, "And if you think that kiss left any lingering effect on me, well I got news for you, asshole—it didn't!"

He laughs out loud, which only pisses me off more. *First Ice, then Hawk, and now this douchebag. I'm really getting sick of the men in my life laughing at me all the time.*

As I walk away, he grabs me by the wrist and pulls me toward him, twisting my arm behind me and holding it at the small of my back. He's got me restrained so close to him, but I refuse to look at him. "Look at me," he demands. I want to ignore his request, but he's so fucking dominant that I can't help but listen. I really hate that about him.

I reluctantly do what he says. As I turn my face up toward his, he says, "Get this straight, Feisty Pants. You will kiss me again, and I guarantee that one day real soon you will be in my bed." He takes his free hand and caresses my cheek. "I don't know why you're fighting this, darling," he looks down at my boots and continues, "because we're gonna be knocking boots before you know it." I'm breathless from his words; even though my mind is saying no, no, no, my libido is screaming yes, yes, yes. My fucking body betrays me every time he's close and it makes me so damn mad at him and myself.

He releases my arm and I step away from him. Catching my breath, I finally get my wits about me. "You know what I guarantee, Sainte?" I get in his face and say, "It will be a cold day in hell before that ever happens." I turn to walk out of the kitchen and then say back to him, "I'll have a grocery list to you shortly." As I walk away I can hear him chuckle quietly. *Asshole!*

It turned out that I only needed a few things for dinner, so when Emma woke up from her nap, she and Sainte went to the store. They got back a few minutes ago.

"Hey Honey, need any help?" Emma asks as she walks into the kitchen, Sainte following closely behind her. What is with him, he's always fucking with her. He's like a damn puppy dog following her around. And speaking of puppies, she's got Hobbes snuggled in her arms.

"Nope, I've got it all under control, Emma, thanks," I reply as I walk over and pet the dog. He really is a cutie. It doesn't matter how mad I am, when I see his adorable face I melt and all the anger goes with it. Damn pup!

She puts Hobbes in my arms and he begins to lick my face. Yep, damn pup. I can't help but giggle as he squirms in my arms. Emma walks over to his food bowl, picks it up and proceeds to feed the little guy. He watches her curiously, patiently waiting for his dinner. I catch a glimpse of Sainte out of the corner of my eye and find him staring as usual. But this is different. Usually when he stares it is predatory, animalistic, and downright arousing. But this time his smile is soft and not sinister. He has a twinkle in his eye; it's like looking into a crystal ball and seeing a softer side of the man that makes me insane.

I give him my best "I'm on to you" look and he smirks. Emma comes back and takes Hobbes from my arms and brings him to his food bowl. Sainte walks over to me and leans in close, then says,

"Chemistry," and walks out of the room. That's all he has to say and that one word pisses me off more than anything because I know he's right. I really hate it when he's right!

Just as I'm finishing up dinner, in walk Hawk and Vince. They're the last ones to arrive. Ari and Rebel returned a little bit ago. Rebel is definitely healing and thanks to nurse Ari, he's getting stronger every day. Ryder, Spike, and Doc arrived right before Hawk and they are now sitting in the living room with Ari and Rebel. Emma and Sainte took Hobbes for a short walk.

When Emma and Sainte return, we all take our seats at the table. Everyone is busy getting their food and making small talk. Hawk politely interrupts and says, "I'm sure you all are wondering why I arranged for this family dinner." The guys look around curiously and nod. "Well, Vince here has some good news and I want him to share it with you all." He looks over at Vince and says, "Vince?"

"Thanks, Hawk. Well, as you all know, I have been spending a lot of time on Ice's case and I am happy to report that they are dropping the charges. No body, no weapon, no evidence, except for Russo's accusation. Frankly, I don't even know why they arrested him in the first place with what they had. Russo must have some pull in this town. But anyway, the good news is that he should be home in a couple of days, once all the paperwork is filed."

The guys cheer and I am surprised to see the relief on Emma's face. I actually thought she would be disappointed. Having Ice back will definitely infringe on her Sainte time.

I am over the moon that Ice is coming home. This club needs him. He's the glue that holds everything together. Although Hawk does a good job at the helm, I just feel that we are all lost and wandering without Ice.

"And, I have another announcement," Hawk adds. "The Vitalis have invited us to New York for Michael Vitali's Omerta."

"What the fuck is an Omerta?" Spike asks.

Vince laughs and says, "Omerta is a code that Italian families in our business hold very dear. It's a code of silence, especially when dealing with the law." He chuckles and says, "I'm sure you all know what I mean." They guys laugh. He then continues, "But in this case, the Vitalis use the Omerta as a rite of passage as well. Domenic, the current Don, is retiring and Michael, his eldest son, is taking over the family. So, we do it the only way we know how, with a party."

I can see the irritation on Hawk's face and I know why. This is a little too much information with us ladies being present. Before Vince continues, Hawk speaks up and says, "I think that is enough, Vince. We don't discuss business with the ladies."

"Oh hell, I'm sorry, Hawk. I wasn't thinking," Vince replies.

Before they can say more, I chime in and ask, "We're all going?"

Hawk says, "Not everyone. I need some of the boys to hang back and keep a handle on things. Spike, I want you to plan on going. Doc assures me that Rebel should be able to ride in a couple of days, so Rebel and Ari, you both will be going." He looks over at me and says, "Of course, you will be riding with me. So ladies, make sure you are prepared for a couple of days on the road."

Well, I was not expecting to be included, but I think it will be nice to get away for a bit. And, hopefully, Sainte will not return with us and crawl back into his hole in New York. It will also give Hawk and I some time together. Ever since our argument the other day, things have been strained between us and it concerns me.

CHAPTER 30

Things are starting to look up. Ice is coming home. Sainte is leaving. Rebel is healed. Finally, we will get things back to normal and I, for one, am thrilled. The last few weeks have been awful.

Today is the day that Ice comes home. We are planning a big welcome home party and dinner for the entire club here at the house. Everyone has been pitching in getting things ready, even Sainte. Sometimes I look at him and think that maybe I didn't give him enough credit. But then I realize that it's a lot easier to be nice to him and give him the benefit of the doubt knowing that his ass will be gone soon and I won't have to deal with him anymore. Life is good.

I made homemade lasagna the other night in preparation for the party and now I am taking the pans out of the freezer so that we can get them in the oven. Hawk went to pick up Ice and they should be here any minute. I can't wait to see him. The guys have been trickling in and Emma and Ari are keeping them happy with beers and snacks. Sainte walks into the kitchen just as I'm pulling a pan from the freezer.

"Here, let me help you with that," he says as he rushes to take the heavy pan from me. His hand grazes against my own and for a brief minute, I can feel the electricity between us. It's really unnerving how he affects me. Realizing that it's best not to give any indication of what I just felt because he would never let it go, I step away from him and allow him to place the pan into the oven.

I walk over to the sink, my back to him, and I can feel him approaching. He stands behind me and leans in against my ear. "Tell me you didn't feel that," he whispers, his breath causing featherlike touches against my skin.

I quickly step away and say, "I have no idea what you're talking about."

"Yeah, darling, keep denying it," he says and then turns to leave. As he walks out of the kitchen, he adds, "It's only gonna make it so much hotter when it does happen. And it's gonna happen."

Oooh, that man infuriates me. What was I saying about him being not so bad? I was so wrong! So very wrong!

The minute Ice walks back into the house, the uneasiness that I have been feeling dissipates. Hawk is back to his old self, and even the rest of the guys seem more at ease. It's funny how one person can ground so many. It's great having him back, but the best part of Ice being back is that Sainte will be leaving. That thought alone puts me in a fantastic mood.

We all sit down for dinner and it really is just like old times. The guys are talking shit and having fun. Sainte doesn't say much, but I catch him looking at me several times and it makes me nervous. I keep telling myself over and over again that he is leaving and that I only have to deal with his smugness for a little while longer.

"So, Wednesday, we'll be leaving for New York," Hawk says.

"Oh, that's right. The Omerta," Ice replies.

"Something is brewing with our friend in New York. Michael requested backup, so Rebel and Spike are going as well," Hawk says.

Ice nods. "That works."

I'm eagerly waiting to hear what is brewing, but the conversation about New York stops. Then Sainte chimes in, "Ice, I'd like a minute with you after dinner, if you don't mind."

"We can do that. I need to talk to you too," Ice says and he almost sounds cold. Suddenly, I'm excited. Ice must have thought about what I told him and he's gonna rip this asshole a new one. *Oh, to be a fly on the wall for that!*

When dinner is over, the girls and I clean up and the guys head out to the pool table and game area. When we are done, we leave the kitchen just as Ice and Sainte are coming out of Ice's office. They're laughing. *What the fuck? Why are they laughing?*

"Hey everyone, got some good news!" Ice yells over all the talking. When everyone quiets down, he says, "We're gaining a new member. Sainte has decided to join the club and I, for one, couldn't be more pleased."

No! No, no no! No fucking way! This was not supposed to happen. Ice was supposed to kick him out. He should be packing his bags!

Hawk walks over to Sainte and pats him on the back. "Welcome, brother. So glad to see that you got smart and decided to hang with the big boys," he says and laughs. *They're happy—all of them. Even Emma and Ari. What the fuck!*

I watch these people that have been family to me for many years now and I feel like I don't know them anymore. Why would they let this troublemaker into our family? I don't get it. As I look around the room, I'm dumbfounded. Then I make eye contact with Sainte and I realize that he's been staring at me the whole time. I can't take any more, so I leave the party and go to my room. I can't watch this fiasco anymore.

Later, when I am sure that everyone has left, I proceed downstairs. I need something to drink, and even wine isn't gonna cut it. I walk over to the bar and pour myself some bourbon. I've never had bourbon before, but Ice drinks it all the time. *How bad can it be?* Besides, I need something strong. Pouring my first shot,

I down it. *Holy shit! I can't fucking breath! My throat is on fire and I feel like I am going to self-combust. How can he drink this stuff?* But instead of backing down and not having any more, I pour myself a second one. The burn isn't so bad the second time around. And just like that, my years of sobriety just went down the drain. Well fuck, a girl can only take so much.

"Don't you think you've had enough?" Sainte says behind me.

Doesn't this guy ever sleep? "What do you want, Sainte?" I'm annoyed.

"Well, I thought that was obvious," he replies.

"Well surprise, Mr. Confident, I don't want you!" I spit.

"You know what, Honey? You're blind. You are so dead-set on hating me that you neglect to see how perfect I am for you."

"Ha! Hawk is perfect for me. You don't know what you're talking about."

"I know you better than you know yourself. Hawk is safe. He's honorable, steadfast, and strong. Who wouldn't love him? But he lacks the one thing I can give you."

"Oh, and what's that?"

"Unbridled passion. I can light that fire in you that you crave, but are too afraid to go after." He takes a step closer, wrapping his arm around my waist he pulls me against him. "All teasing and kidding aside, Honey, I'm what you need. Deep down, even though you are afraid to admit it, I'm the one you want."

I try to push him away, but his grip on me is tight and I'm not strong enough to break free. "I'm not afraid of anything, Sainte. You're delusional."

"Ok, fair enough. Then let's test my theory out." He pauses, waiting for me to respond, but I don't. I'm listening so I can show him he's wrong. "You let me kiss you. You give in to the kiss, no holding back. If, when the kiss is over, you can honestly say that you don't want me, I'll leave you alone. And to sweeten the deal, I'll even leave the MC." He pauses again, then adds, "But if you can't, then I'm staying ... and you and I are going to see where this goes."

Knowing how much I hate him, I quickly agree. I stand there waiting for him to kiss me, and when he doesn't I look at him with confusion. "What? You afraid now?"

"Oh, hell no, darling. I'm planning. This may very well be the last time I kiss you and I'm gonna make sure it's a good one."

"Oh my God, you are really something."

He doesn't answer but begins to back me against the wall. His eyes never leave my own and his stare is so intense I feel as if I am mesmerized. When I hit the wall, he takes my arms and raises them above my head, pinning them there with his right hand. He then takes his left hand and trails it down the center of my body. I begin to squirm. He moves in and tenderly kisses behind my ear and trails kisses down my neck. He moves to my mouth and hovers there briefly, then takes my lips, slowly and passionately at first and then increasing with urgency as he devours my mouth. I can't fight him. I don't want to fight him. I can't deny that he kisses unlike any man I've known and he makes me hungry for more. His tongue begins to dance with mine as he drinks from me, greedily. When he breaks away, I'm breathless, and my lips are swollen and bruised.

He steps backs and says, "Looks like I'm staying," and walks away. I stand there shakily for a few minutes; my legs have turned into rubber bands. *How could one kiss take so much out of me?* When I turn to head back toward the stairs, I find Hawk standing in the hallway. *Fuck!*

"Hawk! I didn't know you were there."

"Obviously," he says and turns to leave.

"Hawk, wait! Let me explain," I call after him.

"I can't talk to you right now. I'm going home. We'll talk in the morning."

"But ..."

"I can't." He turns toward the door and leaves without a glance back toward me.

Oh God, what have I done?

CHAPTER 31

Hawk has been weird since the other night. He refused to talk to me the next morning as he promised. I've tried to talk to him several times after that, but he keeps brushing me off. I know he's pissed and hurt and frankly, I can't blame him. I know what I did was wrong on so many levels. I'm just hoping that once he lets me explain, he'll understand.

We're leaving for New York today. I really want to stay home, but Emma has really pushed for me to go. I'm not comfortable going without talking to Hawk first, so I'll make a point to do that before we get on the road.

Everything is packed. We're only staying a few days, so Ice has instructed all of us to pack light as we're taking the bikes. Luckily for us girls, Hawk, Ice, and Rebel have luggage racks for their bikes. I assume I am still riding with Hawk.

About an hour before we're scheduled to leave, Hawk and Spike show up and begin taking bags out to the bikes. When they are done, I say to Hawk, "Before we leave, can we talk?"

"Honey, not now."

He turns to walk away and I grab his arm. "Nope, not gonna work. We're talking before I get on that bike with you." He looks down at my hand on his arm and I say, "Surely you can spare me a few minutes."

He shakes his head in disgust and says, "Fine." I tug on his arm to follow me and we proceed up the stairs to my room. Once we're behind closed doors he says, "Ok, talk."

"I want to talk to you about the other night."

"I figured as much."

"Look, I'm not sure what you heard or saw, but I want to make it clear that I don't want Sainte. Actually, I can't stand the asshole."

"And what about Ice?"

"We're friends."

"You seem more than friends to me. Not from him, but from you. You've spent so much time over the last couple of weeks worrying about him and Emma, as if you had a vested interest on whether their relationship succeeded or failed."

"The only vested interest I have is that I thought Emma was cheating on him."

"That's what you keep telling yourself, but that isn't the case, is it? You still have feelings for him, and you need to deal with those feelings."

"I'm not in love with him, not the way you think. You don't get it—he saved me. He gave me a home, a job, and a fucking family. I feel as if I owe him, or that we have some sort of bond, he and I."

"The only bond you have with him is friendship and you need to accept that. You spend too much time worrying about his life, his relationship with Emma, and her relationship with Sainte. It's a fucking triangle and there is no room for me in it. And frankly, I'm tired of watching it."

He sits down on the bed and begins to rub at his temples. I sit down next to him and take his hand. "Hawk, I don't want either of them. I want you."

He looks over to me and I can see a sadness in his eyes. "Because I'm safe?"

"You say that as if it is a bad thing."

"Isn't it?" he says sadly.

"No, it's not."

"You know what I think?"

"No, I don't, but whatever it is, you're wrong."

He laughs. "You don't know what you want. You've been in love with Ice for so long, you don't know how to love someone else. And then Sainte comes along with all his charms and you just don't know how to handle him. So you get defensive with him and use hate to push him away. Hate is a very strong emotion. I believe he scares you and so yes, you gravitate to me because I am safe. But I don't want to be safe. I want the woman I love to look at me with fire and passion in her eyes. I want her to look at me the way you look at him. I want a woman who will kiss me as passionately as you kissed Sainte the other night."

"So you saw the kiss?"

"Yes, I did, and it made me realize that you and I will never have that passion. I love ya, but maybe because you're safe for me too."

"So we're not even going to give us a chance and see where this goes?"

He shakes his head. "We're not. I know in my heart that it would be a waste of time. After watching you and Sainte the other night, I truly believe he is the man for you."

"But I hate him." I hear what Hawk is saying and I want to show him that he's wrong, but something inside is screaming at me that he is dead on.

"If you kiss all the men you hate like that, maybe I should make you hate me," he says ruefully.

"I could never hate you." I pause and say, "Maybe if we try harder?"

"Sweetheart, love doesn't require us to try harder. Love is passion. It's all-consuming and I won't settle for anything less."

He's breaking my heart, but he's right. The passion between us is not there, not like it was with Ice and definitely not like it is with Sainte. Hawk is my best friend, my safe haven and he knows me so well, sometimes better than myself. That last thing I want to do is hurt him, but I've already done that.

"He scares me, Hawk," I admit. I see that he is relieved that I finally get what he's saying.

"Baby, you are a strong woman. You are loyal to the core and you love fiercely. You can handle him."

"I'm so afraid he will destroy me."

"Remember when you came to us, how you were so afraid to face the demons of your past? You gradually overcame your fear. You've even faced Briggs. If you can handle all that, you can handle Sainte. I truly believe he is the one for you and I am telling you to give him a chance. I'll always be here for you and I'll always be your best bud. I promise."

I can't stop the tears from falling. I'm such a fool. Hawk is such a good man. He's honorable and loving, and I am letting him walk away. But I understand what he's saying. If it were me, I wouldn't want someone to love me because I was safe. I want the passion he keeps talking about. I want the all-consuming love. I had the passion with Ice, but never the love. Maybe with Sainte, I can have both.

"You are one in a million, you know that." I nudge his shoulder. "I was just thinking that I am such a fool to let you walk away."

"Darl'n', I'm not walking away. I'm letting you find what you crave. I'm smart enough to know that I'm not it. And I'm ok with that."

"And you promise you will still be my bud?"

"I promise." He takes his finger and crosses his heart and I can't help but smile at the gesture. "Now, let's get downstairs and get on the road. I'm sure Ice is champing at the bit to get out of here."

"Ok." We head for the door and I ask, "Am I still riding with you?"

"Of course. I wouldn't want it any other way."

TO BE CONTINUED …

WHY RESCUE?

Saving one dog will not change the world
But surely, for that one dog the world would change forever.

Each year, 2.7 million adoptable dogs and cats are euthanized in the United States alone, simply because too many pets come into shelters and too few people consider adoption when looking for a pet. The number of euthanized animals could be reduced dramatically if more people adopted pets instead of buying them. Next time you are looking for a furry friend, please consider adopting from a reputable rescue.

Not in the market for a pet? You can still make a difference by making a donation to a local rescue, or my rescue of choice, Wolf Spirit Sled Dog Rescue, Inc. (WSSDR).

Wolf Spirit Sled Dog Rescue, Inc. is a 501c3 non-profit rescue located in Stuart, Virginia. Officially opened in August 2013. All WSSDR animals are vetted and micro chipped prior to adoption. They work solely from donations and support from people like you and me. They accept monetary donations, items, and you can even sponsor one of their fur kids If you would like to know more about how you can help please see their donations page on their website.

WOLFSPIRITSLEDDOGRESCUE.ORG

HOBBES

RAW HONEY PLAY LIST

Be Alright by Dean Lewis

Love of My Life by Queen

A Million Dreams by Pink

I Was Born to Love You by Queen

Wild Hearts Can't Be Broken by Pink

I Was Made for Lovin' You by KISS

Promises in the Dark by Pat Benatar

Beautiful Trauma by Pink

Bitch by Meredith Brooks

She's Always a Woman by Billy Joel

Whatever You Want by Pink

ACKNOWLEDGMENTS

As always, I would like to thank my friends and family. Without their support, I never would've had the courage and the vision to become a writer.

I would like to thank my husband Kevin. You've never doubted me or my abilities. All that I am - you let me be. I love you to the moon and back!

Also, I would like to thank the members of my street team, Amy's Amazing Street Girls. You ladies rock my world and I am so honored to have you all on my side.

I'd also like to thank Maureen Goodwin, Ann Lopez and Stephanie Nix. Thank you both so much for being my BETAs on this book and all your help and promotion throughout the publishing process.

I would also like to thank Alicia Freeman and Monica Diane. Your PR abilities are amazing and I couldn't ask for two better personal assistants. You ladies are a pleasure to work with and I could not be more grateful for all that you do for me.

And finally, I would like to thank Ellie and Carl Augsburger of Creative Digital Studios for their insightful ideas, creative cover designs, marketing materials, promotional trailer and comprehensive editing. I am blessed to have such a talented creative design and editing team. You both are top notch!

ABOUT THE AUTHOR

ROMANCES WITH HEART

Amy Cecil is bestselling and award-winning Indie author of both historical and contemporary romance. Her penchant for Austen fan fiction, won her the title of Favorite Historical Romance Author (2016-2017) while her MC series has won several awards throughout the Indie community. Recently, she has expanded her repertoire to the thriller and erotic genres.

For as long as she can remember, Amy always had a book (or two) that she was reading for the love of getting lost within its pages. Amy has been heard to have said, "I've never given much thought to becoming a writer myself until I realized that if I hadn't written my own version of Mr. Darcy, I might have run out of material to read."

And thus, her first novel was born, A Royal Disposition. In the words of Miss Austen herself, "I wish as well as everybody else to be perfectly happy; but, like everybody else, it must be in my own way." Ms. Cecil writes to do just that.

She lives in North Carolina with her husband, Kevin, and their four dogs. When she isn't creating her next masterpiece, or traveling the country for book signings, she enjoys spending time with her husband, friends, and of course her fur babies.

"Face life as you find it-defiantly and unafraid." –Nietzsche

Amazon: www.amazon.com/Amy-Cecil
Goodreads: www.goodreads.com/authoramycecil
BookBub: www.bookbub.com/profile/amy-cecil
Webpage: acecil65.wixsite.com/amycecil
Facebook: www.facebook.com/authoramycecil

AMY'S STREET TEAM

AMY'S AMAZING STREET GIRLS

Are you a member of Amy's street team? If not, you should be! We have all kinds of fun with free reads, sneak peeks, exclusives, games and a weekly SWAG BAG giveaway! Join us!
www.facebook.com/groups/201903646918497/

AMY'S READER/SPOILER GROUP FOR THE KNIGHTS OF SILENCE MC SERIES:

Love spoiler groups... then join us for all Knights talk, including character interviews and special events.
www.facebook.com/groups/510758405985409/

SIGN UP FOR AMY'S NEWSLETTER AND BE IN THE KNOW ON ALL HER LATEST NEWS!

facebook.us15.list-manage.com/subscribe?u=e647cdd64831e6b43a7f279fd&id=7477458db0

OTHER BOOKS BY
AMY CECIL

HISTORICAL ROMANCE

A Royal Disposition:
mybook.to/ARoyalDisposition

Relentless Considerations:
mybook.to/RelentlessConsiderations

On Stranger Prides:
myBook.to/OnStrangerPridesbyAmyCecil

Ripper:
mybook.to/ripperbyamycecil

The Man in the Mirror:
mybook.to/MirrorbyAmyCecil

Mind of a Killer (*Ripper* Prequel)
Coming 2019

On Familiar Prides
Coming 2020

Badass Bikers, Hot Chicks and Sexy Romances.

CONTEMPORARY AND EROTICA ROMANCES

ICE:
mybook.to/ICEbyAmyCecil

ICE ON FIRE:
mybook.to/ICEonFIREbyAmyCecil

CELTIC DRAGON:
mybook.to/CELTICDRAGONbyAmyCecil

FORGETTING THE ENEMY – Book 1:
mybook.to/FTEbyAmyCecil

LOVING THE ENEMY – Book 2:
Releasing May 9, 2019

SAINTE:
Releasing 2020

Don't Forget …

If you've read *Raw Honey* and loved it, then please leave a review. Authors love reading reviews!

Made in the USA
Columbia, SC
17 March 2019